ABOUT THIS BOOK

Heidi Bennett had the perfect life—including great parents and an insanely romantic boyfriend—until it all came to a screeching halt the night of the Cold Moon Ball last December. Now, months after her disappearance, Heidi walks among the residents of Havenwood Falls once again, but most—whether human or supernatural—can't see her.

The last thing Heidi remembers was dancing with her boyfriend at the ball. Her disappearance, and the events surrounding it, remain a complete mystery. One she's determined to solve.

Zane is a guardian angel with a history of making questionable choices. As punishment for one such decision, he's ordered to stay with Heidi while she fulfills her mission. But he struggles with his choices yet again when he finds himself in the middle of a dangerous game—a game whose outcome could have eternal consequences not only for him, but for Heidi as well. And only one of them can win.

AVENOIR

A HAVENWOOD FALLS HIGH NOVELLA

DANIELE LANZAROTTA

HAVENWOOD FALLS HIGH BOOKS

Written in the Stars by Kallie Ross

Reawakened by Morgan Wylie

The Fall by Kristen Yard

Somewhere Within by Amy Hale

Awaken the Soul by Michele G. Miller

Bound by Shadows by Cameo Renae

Inamorata by Randi Cooley Wilson

Fata Morgana by E.J. Fechenda

Forever Emeline by Katie M. John

Reclamation by AnnaLisa Grant

Avenoir by Daniele Lanzarotta

Avenge the Heart by Michele G. Miller

Curse the Night by R.K. Ryals (August 2018)

Blood & Iron by Amy Hale (September 2018)

More books releasing on a monthly basis.

Stay up to date at www.HavenwoodFalls.com

ALSO BY DANIELE LANZAROTTA

Academy of the Fallen Series – YA

Wide Awake

Nephilim

Sins of the Fallen

Forsaken

Sudden Hope Novels – YA

Sudden Hope

Catch Me If I Fall

Imprinted Souls Series – YA

Imprinted Souls

Bloodlust

Divine Ashes

Blood Bound

Shattered Souls

Reawakening Series – YA

Venom

Blood Ties (Coming 2019)

A Mermaid's Curse Trilogy – Adult

Insatiable

Fated

Unbreakable

Individual Titles

The Right Kind of Wrong – Adult

Published by

Ang'dora Productions, LLC

5621 Strand Blvd, Ste 210

Naples, FL 34110

Cover design by Regina Wamba at MaelDesign.com

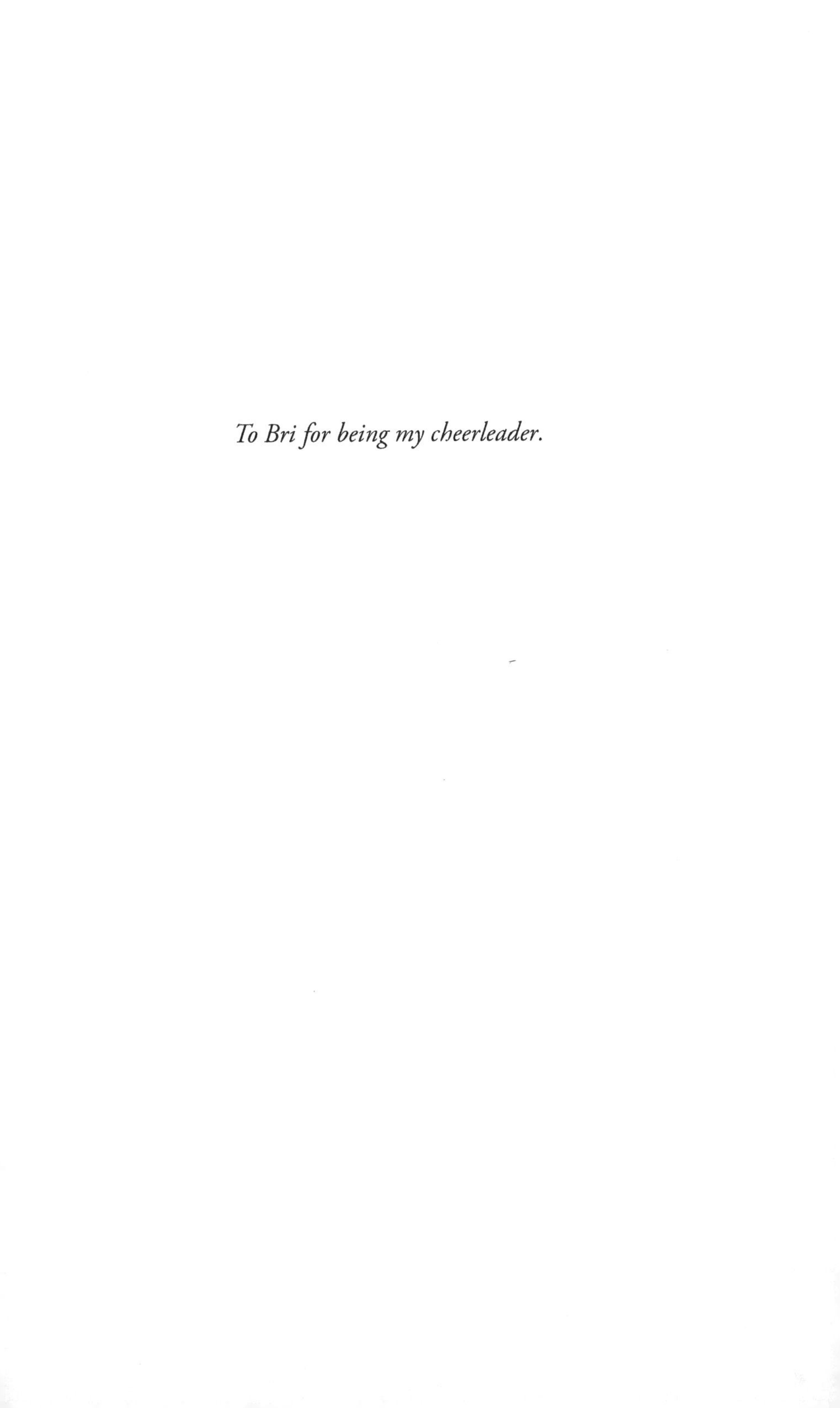

To Bri for being my cheerleader.

PROLOGUE

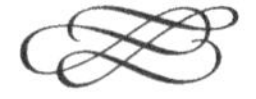

DECEMBER 2017

I look at my reflection in the mirror, and I think about backing out of the Cold Moon Ball for the hundredth time. Tonight should feel perfect. This is one of my favorite events in Havenwood Falls. My long light-blue dress is absolutely stunning, and Mom insisted that I borrow this beautiful silver crown she won at a pageant, but none of it takes my mind away from this gut feeling that something bad is going to happen.

"You look beautiful," Mom says. I turn around, and she's leaning against the doorframe, keeping her distance, as she has been sick over the past few days.

I bite my bottom lip, feeling uncertain about this whole night.

"What's going on?" she asks.

I take a deep breath and glance down toward the infinity symbol on the promise ring Jace gave me last year for my sixteenth birthday. Without taking my eyes off the ring, I say what has been on my mind since last night, when I talked to him. "Jace said he needs to talk to me about something important."

Mom tilts her head to the side and gives me a reassuring smile. "I hope you don't think he's breaking up with you. You two have been together since middle school, and you get along better than most adult couples I know." She laughs.

I feel myself relax. She's right. I've just never heard him sound so serious before.

The doorbell rings, and Mom smiles again. "I'll get it. I'll let him know you will be down in a bit."

I look at the mirror one more time, take a deep breath, and tell myself to get it together.

As I walk out of my room, I see Jace at the bottom of the stairs, with his back to me. He's wearing black pants and a black peacoat. I can almost guarantee that instead of a dress shirt, he's wearing an old band T-shirt under his coat. The thought of that makes me laugh for a split second, before that gut feeling consumes my every thought yet again. As I make my way down the stairs, I even manage to fake a smile. The moment Jace turns around and looks up at me, his mouth hangs open, and I know by the way that he stares at me that Mom is right. Just like that, the fake smile quickly turns into a huge grin.

We say goodbye to my mom and head outside. Jace puts his hand on the small of my back as we walk away, and I freeze in place when I see his dad's black Camaro convertible parked on the street.

"Do you want to drive?" he asks, and my eyes widen.

I laugh and look at him. "You're kidding, right? I'm surprised your dad let you drive his favorite child."

Jace chuckles, showing off his dimples. He always jokes about his dad loving that car more than anything or anyone else.

"There is no way I'm driving it," I say.

He grins at me. "We should get going. We already missed the first part of the evening."

As we drive up toward Havenwood Heights, Jace turns the music up loud, and I find myself distracted by the Christmas decorations along the way. When I was little, Dad used to bring me to this area every Christmas and just drive around. And no matter how many times we did that over the years, the sight of the large houses with Christmas lights glowing, and Mt. Alexa in the background, is always breathtaking.

When we get to the Mills mansion, one of the biggest houses on the street, Jace parks his dad's car as far away as possible from other cars around.

"Wait." He stops me when I reach for the door. He gives me a crooked smile before he gets out and rushes to my side. He opens my door and extends his hand to me. Once out of the car, I see just how far we have to walk. I laugh. "You did have his permission to take the car, right?" I ask jokingly.

Jace chuckles as he slips his hand into mine. "Yep, although he did have a few glasses of wine earlier. Maybe I should've gotten that in writing."

I just shake my head.

"So, what shirt are you wearing tonight?" I ask as we make our way to the door. "Pink Floyd or—"

He cuts me off. "What makes you think I'm not wearing a dress shirt?"

I glare at him, and he grins. "Okay. You got me. And you got it right on the first guess. Not bad." He winks.

Stepping into the ballroom is like being transported into a different world. I stop for a minute to take in the place. The crystal candelabras everywhere and the fresh cut flowers on each of the tables around the room make the ballroom look stunning, just like it does every year. But my favorite part has really always been the large skylight on the ceiling, allowing for the most breathtaking view of the moon. I've always wondered what it would be like to be in this ballroom when it is empty, just laying down on the floor at night, in silence, staring at the moon. Jace nudges my shoulder with his, leans against me, and whispers, "Ready to go, Cinderella?"

I giggle. "Yes."

Jace and I walk toward the tables filled with drinks and appetizers. On the way there, we say hi to a few people from school. I stop to talk to Zoey, Mr. Mills's granddaughter, and wish her a happy birthday. She's new to our school, so I don't know her well, but she seems nice. Minutes later, I catch Jace watching me with this sad look in his eyes. I can see the moment he tenses, and just like that, the gut feeling is back.

Jace walks toward me. "Come with me," he whispers, and he leads me through the double doors that take us to the backyard of the mansion. I'm so nervous, I don't even notice our surroundings. I just know that something bad is coming. Jace reaches for my hand and brushes his finger over the infinity symbol on my ring. He just keeps staring at the ring and playing with it, and my anxiety gets the best of me.

"What did you want to talk about?" I ask in a nervous tone.

He gives me a sad smile. "Later," he says.

He reaches for his phone and plugs his headphones in. I give him a puzzled look, and he smiles. He reaches over and puts the headphones in my ears. Nothing is playing at this point. He leans in and gives me a quick kiss before asking me to dance with him.

I blush and look down, avoiding his gaze. This is so like him, to make these big romantic gestures that I can never say no to.

He gently puts his fingers against my chin, tilting my head up. "Close your eyes," he whispers before he pushes play and one of my favorite slow songs comes on. He closes the distance between us, and my eyes drift shut. After a while, I feel the cold snowflakes falling against my skin, and I grin. But it is his laughter that brings me back to the moment. I open my eyes to find him watching me with a grin across his face—showing off his dimples—and there is this sparkle in his eyes.

I memorize every single detail—every single feeling about this moment. The cold. The few seconds of snow, just at the right time. His smile. That look in his eyes. It's almost as if I'm programming myself to memorize everything about this one happy moment.

As if it was my last.

CHAPTER 1

HEIDI

MAY 2018

"Jace," I mumble as I open my eyes.

Feeling disoriented, I realize that I'm lying face down on dirt and grass. *Snow . . . What happened to the snow?* I sit, slowly, and look up. The first thing I see is the moon. My head is spinning like crazy. At the sound of something howling, I frantically stand up and look around for my phone. I curse myself for having a black phone case.

"Ugh. I'm never going to find the thing in the dark."

I hear the sound of someone clearing his throat, and for a split second, I feel myself relax, thinking that it is Jace. I spin around—faster than I should—and see a tall dark-haired guy with bright green eyes, leaning against a tree right before me.

"Need help finding something?" he asks with a raspy voice, crossing his arms over his chest.

I take a step back. "Who are you?"

He shrugs and just keeps gawking at me. I haven't seen him at school before. He is the kind of person I would remember seeing. Something about him feels . . . different.

"I'm leaving," I say, and I feel stupid for even having to announce that. I should be running, but my still-spinning head is a huge sign I wouldn't make it far. I turn around and start to walk away slowly, and hope to God he doesn't follow me. *Ugh. I'm always making fun of people in scary movies who try to run and end up getting killed. Please don't let me become a cliché.*

I don't get far before I hear him again.

"Wrong way," he says.

I glance back, and he is at the exact same spot. He points in a completely different direction. I find myself questioning whether to believe him or not, but another howl coming from the direction I'd been heading makes me follow his guidance. I give him a short nod and start walking away. As soon as I'm far enough from his view, I pick up the pace, and with every step, I feel like something is behind me—until I'm out of the woods.

Somehow, I find my way out to where I can see the Mills estate. I keep walking, and I don't stop until I'm in front of the mansion. I stare at it—probably for longer than I should, considering that something is definitely not right. I look down at the long light-blue dress I wore to the ball, then back at the mansion. You can't even tell something happened here tonight. *His smile . . . the snow . . .* I look around, confused. Strange things happen in this town from time to time, but nothing like this. How many hours could have passed?

"My parents are going to freaking ground me for life," I mumble before I turn around and head home.

As I make my way down Eighth Street, it hits me that the Christmas decorations are gone. I shake my head and keep walking. I replay the night in my head over and over. The last thing I remember was Jace and me dancing. He'd have never let me go into those woods alone. When I get to town square, chills creep over my skin. I feel like someone is watching me again, and I start to walk faster. I'm pretty much running by the time I arrive at my front door.

I stop in front of my house and sigh. I reach for the doorknob and slowly turn it, thankful that my parents never lock the door. If I'm lucky enough, they're sleeping.

I slowly close the door behind me. The house is pitch black. *Yes!* I think to myself.

I go straight upstairs to my room. I open the door and wonder where this god-awful lavender smell is coming from. I look at the clock, and it is three in the morning. I think about calling Jace to find out what happened, but remember that my phone is gone. I'm definitely not taking the risk of waking up mom and dad just to use their phones. Without even turning the lights on or bothering to change, I just make my way to bed and lie down. My first thought is that the mattress feels weird, but I quickly dismiss it as me possibly being tired—even though I don't feel tired at all. And then, I turn around and see the shape of a body next to me. I scream bloody murder as I jump up and rush to turn the light on. A familiar girl lies on my bed.

"Rose?" I say. "Hey!" I yell at my cousin.

Nothing. She doesn't even move.

I start to tremble as I walk closer to my bed. I poke her arm once, then again—really hard. She just tosses and turns.

I turn around to go get Mom, but freeze in place when I see my reflection in the mirror. Barely recognizing myself, I take a few steps closer and lean in toward the mirror. My dress is covered in dirt and blood. My gaze goes to the gash on my forehead with dried-up blood surrounding it. The skin around it looks discolored. I lean even closer and lightly touch the gash on my forehead. I feel nothing, and that is when I realize that I must be having one screwed-up dream. This has to be a dream . . .

I poke at the gash on my forehead again. Harder this time.

"That is disgusting." It's the same voice I heard back in the woods, and I spin around to see that guy again. "You won't feel anything," he says as he yawns and sits on my bed.

I should be scared of him. I should be yelling or running, or both, but I feel oddly calm. And honestly, I'm just waiting to wake up at any second and make this all go away.

I glance at Rose, and she's in a deep sleep.

"She can't hear us," he says. His tone is dry and cold, but I can see concern in the way he's watching me, and my stomach drops.

"I'm not dreaming, am I?" I ask, and he shakes his head. I look back at the mirror and stare. "What happened to me?" I whisper, feeling the need to cry, but unable to.

Looking in the mirror, I see him walk closer and stand right next to me. His gaze holds mine through our reflections.

"You died," he says.

My knees weaken, and I lose my balance. When his arms inch toward me, I stop him.

"Get away from me," I say as I regain my balance.

He puts his hands up and steps back with this hurt look in his eyes.

"Who are you?" I ask frantically.

He lowers his head and runs his fingers through his dark hair before he looks back at me.

"My name is Zane, and I'm an angel," he says in a serious tone.

I just stare at him before I burst into laughter, and he gives me a confused look. When I manage to stop laughing, I watch him and tilt my head to the side. Maybe this is not real after all. "I've had messed up dreams before, but this tops them all."

"I didn't lie before. It's not a dream," he says.

Still laughing, I roll my eyes at him. "Do you mean you are a guardian angel? Because if so, you sure are doing a lousy job at it," I say as I point toward my forehead.

"I didn't say I was *your* guardian angel," he says in an annoyed tone.

My laughter vanishes. "Why are you here?" I ask.

"I was sent to help you."

"Help me with what?" I ask.

"You died before your time. You have a mission to fulfill before you can move on," he says, sounding even more annoyed than he did seconds before.

I frown as I glance back toward the mirror.

"What happened to me?"

He pauses for a while. "I don't know. Like I said, I'm not your guardian angel."

I turn around, cross my arms, and tap my foot on the carpet. "Don't you people communicate?"

He smirks and shakes his head. He looks like a completely different guy when he loses that serious look and cold tone.

"I hate that habit of yours," he says, and when I give him a puzzled look, he goes on. "The habit of making jokes when you are afraid, or sad, or stressed."

"You know me," I say, and he ignores me completely.

"To answer your question, angels do communicate, but we don't have all the answers. And I'm here as punishment and training."

I tilt my head to the side. "So not only do I get sent an angel that is not mine, I get sent one who doesn't know what he's doing. No wonder I'm dead!" I know I'm seconds away from falling apart. He's right. I always use humor to deflect the real stuff. I close my eyes for a split second. "If guardian angels are really real, where is mine?" I ask.

He sits back down on my bed. For the first time, I take a good look at him. The faded jeans, black T-shirt, combat boots . . . He doesn't look like an angel—at all.

"I wish I knew," he says, returning to his dry tone. "And for the record, I know what I am doing."

The snow . . .

"How long have I been . . . dead?" I ask.

He just sits there, staring at me, and I know he's not going to answer.

"Get out," I snap.

"But I am supposed to—"

"You haven't been very helpful so far. I don't even have proof that you're an angel, or that I am dead. Leave!" I order.

He puts his hands up. "Call me when you need me, and trust me, you will. I won't be far," he growls, before he disappears.

CHAPTER 2

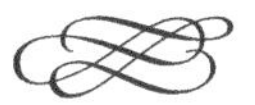

HEIDI

The moment he is gone, I feel lightheaded. I crouch down in the corner of my room. A thousand questions run through my mind. What happened to me? What happened to Jace? How long has it been?

This can't be real. It just can't be! I sit here and stare at Rose. I hug my knees and just stay where I am and watch time go by. I'm in a trance-like state when the sound of my alarm makes me jump.

Rose rolls over, shuts it off, and goes back to sleep. Minutes later, there is a soft knock on the door. The door slowly opens, and my mom's face comes into view, and I lose it—or at least, I feel like I do. I want to cry, but there are no tears.

"Rose, honey. Wake up. Your mom is on her way to get you."

When Rose doesn't move, Mom comes in and walks toward the bed. I'm shocked at how much weight she's lost. Her hair is not done like usual. She wouldn't be caught dead in her natural hair color. In fact, I often joke that she practically lives at Shear Magic. She hates dark hair on her, but now, her hair is pitch black. I slowly stand up. I lose my balance for a split second before I walk toward her.

"Ro—" she starts to say as I step closer to her. I'm right next to her when she closes her eyes and takes a deep breath.

"Mom," I whisper as I reach for her. Only, my hand goes right through hers. I stare at my hand, confused—wondering why, considering that I was able to touch Rose's arm before.

I look back at my mom. She opens her eyes and looks toward the closet door, where she used to mark and measure my height while growing up. She wipes a tear away and rushes out of the room.

I follow her out. I feel stronger as I step out of my room. I keep following as she goes back in her room, crawls into bed, and closes her eyes. She doesn't get back up until my aunt arrives to pick up Rose, and she goes back to bed as soon as they leave.

Feeling like I am being watched, I turn around to find Zane standing against the doorframe. I roll my eyes and let out an annoyed grunt.

"Why are you here?" I growl.

He shrugs. "You need me."

"No, I don't."

He grins and volunteers the first useful piece of information since I first saw him. "Do you know why you felt weak when you sent me away?"

I shake my head. "How do you even know I felt like that?" I ask as I cross my arms.

"You're linked to the place where you died."

My eyes widen at hearing him say that like it's nothing.

"What?" he says. "You already knew you are dead. No big news there. Anyway. If I leave, you go right back to where you died, and I might not be able to find you or get you out, so I can't let that happen."

"I woke up in the woods. Isn't that where I died?" I ask, and he shakes his head. "I was told to go to that area for my next assignment. Another angel brought you to me. What I do know is that your body was never found, and it has been months. I can guarantee that if your body was anywhere in this town, you would've been found by now."

Annoyed, I blurt out, "Okay, so this angel brought me from somewhere. He should know where I am."

He raises his voice. "Trust me. I've asked. I was told it was not my place to have those answers. Point is," he continues, "we're both stuck here until you fulfill your mission."

I let out a frustrated sigh. "What is this mission anyway? Because this sure will go faster if you tell me everything I need to know."

"Can't," he says.

I give him a doubtful look.

"They didn't tell me, okay?"

I notice he is nervous and he can't make eye contact.

"Should angels lie?" I ask, and he looks like I've caught him by surprise. "Tell me the truth," I demand.

He sighs. "As a general rule, you need to find peace by finding out what happened to you."

He still can't make eye contact.

"What else?"

He shrugs. "I may have overheard that something needs to be repaired."

"Where did you hear that?" I ask.

"From the one who brought you to me."

"I'm guessing he orders you around?" I ask, and I notice that he has his hands clenched into fists. "Let me talk to him."

He bursts into laughter. "Oh, I don't think so."

I roll my eyes at him. I wonder why they would send me an angel after I died. Besides, I have yet to see wings. Angels should have wings, or at least I think they should.

I think back to the TV shows I watch—well, used to watch. "Are you some kind of creepy reaper?"

He laughs again. "Come on," he says, motioning for me to follow him, and his refusal to answer my questions irritates me more and more.

"I'm not going until you tell me," I say.

He grins, looking amused, and when I don't move, he says, "No, I'm not a reaper. And no one is even allowed to reap your soul until you fulfill your mission."

I give him a puzzled look.

"Let's face it. You're stuck with me. We might as well start by helping you remember what happened that night."

I sigh. As afraid as I am of finding out, I do want to . . .

I look back at Mom, still in bed. I get close to her.

"I love you, Mom," I whisper in her ear, and she opens her eyes again. I wonder if she can sense me here.

I walk back to my room with Zane following me.

"What are you doing?" he asks.

"Changing out of this dress."

He laughs, and I spin around to face him. "What?"

"No one can even see you. Why bother?"

"You can see me," I say, and he looks embarrassed. "Relax. I'm not trying to impress you, if that is what you're worried about. I just want out of this dress, okay? I need something that feels normal —and something clean. Please," I beg. By the expression on his face, he understands.

I walk into my room and go to my dresser, opening the top drawer. Everything is exactly as I left it.

Standing here, staring at my clothes, I ask, "Do you think they know that I died?" I glance at him, and he looks so lost. "My parents. I know my body was never found, but do you think they know it somehow?" I ask, being clearer this time.

I can see it in his eyes that he feels bad for me. "Your parents hope you're just missing. They haven't stopped looking." He pauses. "Close your eyes," he says, and I raise an eyebrow at him.

"Please," he begs.

I hesitantly close my eyes. Seconds later, I feel his touch against my forehead.

"Okay, open," he says, and his fingers linger against my skin for a moment longer. When he pulls away, he nods toward the mirror.

I look over, and the gash on my forehead is completely gone. I stand here in shock and stare at Zane.

"Thank you," I say. I glance back down at my dresser. "Do you mind leaving?"

"You won't be able to touch those clothes without my help," he says.

I give him a puzzled look.

"Try it," he says with a grin as he walks away and stands right outside of my room.

I do, and my hand goes right through it.

He smiles and closes the distance between us. "Now try again," he says, and this time, I can.

I turn around. "I was able to touch things without you around before," I say.

"I was here. You just couldn't see me."

I laugh. "Well, I'm not changing in front of you."

He turns and faces the wall.

"If you so much as peek at me, I swear . . ."

He doesn't say anything, but I can see the movement of his shoulders, and I can hear him chuckle.

I put my jeans on under the dress. I then unzip and remove the dress and put a tank top and sweater on. "You can turn around," I say as I go to grab my boots.

"You know you can't feel cold, right? Not that it is cold right now."

I shrug. "So? Maybe this is my favorite outfit. If I'm going to be stuck wearing the same thing forever"—I shake my head thinking of how unreal this is—"maybe I want this to be my permanent ghost outfit, okay?"

He laughs and shakes his head as he walks over to my closet. He reaches in, and when he turns around, he is holding a light gray sweater I got for Christmas last year. He throws it toward me.

"You might as well go with a real favorite, then." He winks before he turns back around and walks toward the door.

I put my sweater on.

"Zane?" I say, and he turns around to face me. "Won't people be able to see my clothes?" I ask, confused.

He laughs. "That would be entertaining, wouldn't it?"

I cross my arms and wait on a reply, clearly not amused.

"No," he says. "I have certain abilities. They won't be able to see anything that you wear, or hold."

I shrug and give my room one last look before I follow him.

When I walk by the kitchen, my eyes go straight to the calendar hanging on the wall—May 2018. I stumble back.

"Where have I been this whole time?" I say, raising my voice. Again, Zane says nothing.

I feel sick to my stomach.

"I want to see Jace," I say, and Zane freezes in place as I see fear in his eyes.

CHAPTER 3

HEIDI

"I need to see Jace," I say again when Zane doesn't say anything back.

He shakes his head. "You're not ready to see him."

The look in his eyes makes me feel anxious, and I start to wonder if maybe Jace is with someone else by now. Or even worse. I'm filled with fear at the thought that maybe something happened to him, too. I walk past Zane, making my way out the door. I feel weak as soon as I step outside. I look back, Zane takes a few steps closer, and I feel okay again.

"I told you, you need me close by in order to stay here," he says in a cold tone.

I wait as he approaches.

"Close your eyes," he says, and when I don't, he just shakes his head. He reaches for my wrist, and before I can pull away, he softly wraps his hand around it. Next thing I know, we are back in the woods in what seems to be the area where I woke up.

I wrap my arms around myself. "Why are we here?" I ask.

"To see if you remember anything."

I take a good look around. Nothing. I remember nothing. I just feel agitated and ready to see Jace, even though I'm afraid to. I look down at my ring and close my eyes, remembering when he was playing with it that night. I remember he looked tense.

"You remember something," says Zane.

"Not important," I say, and I swallow the lump in my throat and get the courage to ask, "Why am I not ready to see Jace? He is okay, right?"

He leans his back against a tree like he doesn't have a care in the world. "Because your emotions are going to be all over the place." He pauses. "Even more so than they are right now. I'm not dealing with an unstable ghost."

I raise an eyebrow at him and tilt my head to the side. I'm not even sure if I'm more insulted that he referred to me as a ghost or unstable.

He sighs and lowers his voice. "Look, at least give yourself a day to process, all right? I'll take you to see him then."

"Not like I have a choice," I say in a frustrated tone.

He actually chuckles at my reaction. "Come on," he says. "Let's walk back to the Mills mansion. Maybe you'll remember something."

I nod and start walking with him.

"Can I ask you something?" I say.

"Sure," he says. He doesn't mean that at all, and I doubt he will even answer it.

"Why are you being punished? Is that why you don't have your wings?"

He keeps walking without even looking in my direction. "I have wings. I choose when I want them to be seen."

"And the punishment . . . What did you do?" I ask.

He stops walking then and glares at me. It feels like those green eyes are piercing through my soul. If I even have a soul. "Do I have a soul?" I blurt out.

He laughs. "I thought we covered that when you asked me if I was a reaper." I give him a puzzled look, trying to remember that among the chaos that all of this has been since I woke up. He rolls his eyes. "Your soul is fine . . ."

We get to the back of the mansion, and of course, he doesn't think I noticed how he dodged that question, but I will ask him again soon enough. I stare at the mansion, trying to remember something—anything.

"The last thing I remember was Jace and me dancing in the snow, and laughing," I say.

Zane lets out a frustrated sigh, and I give him a sideways look.

"What?" he asks.

"Oh, nothing. I mean . . . I'm dead and can't remember what happened to me. I think if anyone here has the right to be frustrated, that would be me."

He leans his head down and runs his hand through his hair. "You're right. I'm sorry." He looks back at me. "Let's start over, okay? Maybe if we do something else to take your mind off it, your memories might come to you." He pauses. "Music store?" he suggests, and I actually smile at the thought of it.

Music has always felt like therapy to me, partly because I grew up taking dance classes, but mostly because music is Jace's thing, and I could've spent the rest of my life just listening to him sing.

I think about asking Zane if we can walk to the music store, but before I can even say anything, he is already reaching for my hand, and next thing I know, we are in town square, right in front of Havenwood Falls Music & More. We walk in, and I close my eyes for a split second. The store smells like . . . home. I've always loved living in Havenwood Falls, and this right here is one of my favorite places. I look toward the back and see the owner, Cecelia, talking to someone. Something about seeing the way she moves is so comforting—has always been. For a split second, watching her happiness brings a smile to my face. Her customer thanks her, and when she turns around, facing us, Zane tenses and abruptly blocks my view.

"What was that about?" I ask.

"What?" he asks, as if he doesn't know what I'm referring to. I roll my eyes at him.

I look around for a while, before I decide to just sit on the floor against the wall and people-watch. To be honest, I hope Jace shows up here. He loves this place. Zane sits next to me, blocking part of my view.

Soon, my mind quickly goes back to a much darker place.

I sigh. "Do you think it is best for my parents to keep thinking that I'm just missing or to know the truth?"

He stops to think about it. "Honest?" he asks, and I nod. "I think the truth is always best. It'll be painful, but it'll give them closure."

I glance down for a split second before looking back at him. "I agree. Is there a way to let them know?" I ask, and he looks into my eyes.

"I'll find a way, if that is what you wish."

"Thank you," I say.

It's weird, sitting here, looking at people and listening to their conversations, when they have no idea that I'm here. It somehow doesn't feel intrusive, though. I mean, who am I going to tell their gossip to? Zane and I end up spending the day listening to music and watching people go by. When dinnertime comes around, I can almost picture Mom and Dad sitting down to eat like they always do at six on the dot. When we finally leave the store, it's dark out. I stand in the middle of Town Square Park, watching the streets slowly grow empty as people head home. I look over at Zane. "What now?"

He tilts his head to the side and gives me a puzzled look.

"I assume neither of us needs sleep. What do we do now?" I ask.

He laughs. "We go back to your home until morning."

I feel like my stomach drops. I can't go back there. I can't take seeing that look in my mom's eyes. And my dad . . . I don't think I can take seeing him at all.

"You don't have to see them," he says, as if reading my mind. "I'll make sure it's clear before you go in."

I shake my head. "Why can't we just stay out? There are things we could be doing. Maybe go back to the woods, now that it is dark out, to see if I remember something."

He chuckles. "I don't think so. You're not ready for Havenwood Falls. Not yet, anyway."

I raise an eyebrow at him. "Care to elaborate?" I ask, and he just turns around and starts to walk away. I stay where I am.

After he takes a few steps, he turns back around. "You really don't want to go back to your home?" he asks, and I shake my head.

"Come on. I know a place."

I hesitantly follow him as he leads us through town toward the school, but we stop at the library.

"What? No magical transportation?" I ask, and he laughs.

"Don't get spoiled by my abilities. You won't have them at your disposal forever."

I roll my eyes at him.

We walk into the Victorian style manor that is the new library, and I close my eyes for a split second and focus on the scent of books. My mind becomes overwhelmed with memories of when I was little and Dad used to take me to the old library every week to pick out new books.

"Was this a bad idea?" Zane asks, and for the first time since we met, he sounds genuinely concerned. I don't answer right away, and after a moment, I realize there are tears running down my face. Something I couldn't do before.

Zane gives me a sad smile and shrugs. “Sometimes you just need to feel human for a while,” he says before he turns around.

“Thank you,” I say, following him up the steps.

Once we are upstairs, he turns around to find me sobbing.

“I’ll be looking around if you need anything,” he says uncomfortably.

I give him a short nod, and he walks into one of the rooms. Knowing I can’t go far, I follow him in. I walk around, picking up book after book and putting them back, unable to find something that will keep my attention. My head is such a freaking mess, I know I won’t be able to focus on anything. After a few minutes, I go to the side of the room where he is, and I see him sitting on the floor with his back against the wall, reading a book. Sensing me watching him, he looks up, and I slowly walk toward him.

CHAPTER 4

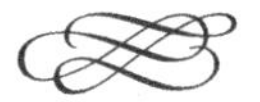

ZANE

I hold Heidi's gaze as she walks toward me.

"Can I sit with you? I don't think I want to be alone," she says.

I nod to the side, and she slowly sinks to the floor next to me.

"What are you reading?" she asks as she looks over.

Not once while she was alive did I ever dream about being able to have a conversation with her, let alone be sitting this close together.

"It's fiction. About angels," I say, and she laughs. The last time I heard her laugh like this, she was with her boyfriend, dancing in the snow. Right before I got pulled away. Right before everything went wrong. They kept me away and in the dark about her being gone until I was given this insane assignment.

She looks over at the book, and I watch her every feature as she reads over the lines, and I get lost in the moment. *I have to stick to the plan—get it together and detach.*

"Here." I hand her the book. "You read it. I'll find something else," I say as I get up.

"I'm sorry. I didn't mean to—I just . . . I read this before. Please stay," she asks.

I sit back down, but move over, putting some distance between us.

"How long have you been an angel?" she asks.

"A little over a century."

Her eyes widen for a split second. "What else would really happen to me if you weren't close by?" she asks. "I feel weak when I walk away. I know I can't touch things. What else?"

I tense. "You'd be able to see some things for what they really are."

She gives me a confused look, but I ignore it. She doesn't need to know about the beings that live here, on top of everything else. She would be a walking mess worrying about her family and Jace.

"When I touch people, can they feel me?"

"If you are intentionally trying to touch them and I'm close by, they might feel the energy, I guess . . . but no, you can't go around poking and hugging humans and make them feel that, if that is what you want to know." He grins. "And unless you are putting a great amount of energy into it, they will just walk right through you, even with me being near."

She looks away for a split second. She was obviously not amused by my attempt at a joke. "What will happen to me if I don't fulfill my mission? If I don't remember what happened or if I don't repair whatever it is that I might need to repair?"

I'm the one avoiding her gaze now. "You'd be stuck here. You'd never move on. You'd just watch people—your parents—get older. People would come and go, and you'd always just be here. That is, assuming I'm allowed to stay with you. Otherwise, you'd be stuck where you died."

I can see the horror in her eyes as she subconsciously touches her forehead, where her injury was.

She does that thing where she jokes to deflect from reality. "So much for sugarcoating the truth." She pauses, waiting for my reaction, and when there is none, she goes on. "What will happen to me if I do what I need to?" she asks.

I shrug. "I assume you'll get peace and all that good heavenly stuff." *And you'll be pulled away from me,* I think to myself and start to shake my head.

She giggles. "Are you sure you are an angel?"

"Why do you ask?" I say.

"There is this bitter tone when you talk about those things."

"I'm sure," I say. "Unfortunately," I whisper under my breath as I get up.

I pull another book out from the shelf.

"I miss Jace," she says in a tone that makes me feel a thousand emotions at once—none of which I should be feeling.

"I suppose it's normal for you to feel that way," I snap before I walk away without looking back at her, because if I do, I know I'm doomed. She'll end up stuck here, and it will be my fault.

CHAPTER 5

HEIDI

Well, this ghost thing is going to get old fast. I spend the night reading books about ghosts of all things, to see if I can identify with anything at all, and also, to escape into someone else's world for a while. I sense Zane watching me every once in a while, but I ignore him, knowing that either he is a complete jerk or he is just not used to people.

When morning comes, I feel nervous like I've never been before.

I walk over to the window on the second floor of the library and watch people go by as they start their day.

"I'm not sure going to the school is a good idea. Maybe you should wait longer," Zane says, startling me.

I didn't even hear him move. I turn around and glare at him. He shakes his head, clearly frustrated that he's stuck here with me. I don't even have to say anything.

"Fine. Are you ready to go?" he asks.

"I could never be ready for this," I say, and I contemplate if seeing Jace is even a good idea at all, but deep inside, I know that I need to. I look back outside. "Just give me a little while before we go."

Zane backs away, and in an attempt to prepare myself to see Jace, I run just about every possible worst-case scenario in my head—the worst of all being that he moved on and is dating someone I know.

Zane doesn't make a sound until I tell him that I'm ready to go.

Going into the school feels like a nightmare. I walk a few steps behind Zane, mostly because I don't feel like talking or seeing his frustrated *I told you so* expression in relation to this being a bad idea. I'm not ready for this at all. The first familiar face I see is Gianna Augustine, and that is when it hits me that I won't be graduating with my class, or doing any of the things I was looking forward to. As the bell rings, I stand at the end of the hallway, feeling sick, and then stunned as people walk literally through me. With each step they take, as they walk through me, something strange happens. I capture a few split seconds of memories, all of them related to me in some way. I close my eyes as I see and listen to them talking to others about me. "Did you hear about Heidi?". . . "Hey. Did you see Heidi last night before she went missing?" And most of them saying, "I heard she ran away."

I look at Zane. I can't even tell if he is irritated or concerned, but without saying a word, he patiently waits until I'm ready to keep going.

"He is in art class," he says.

"How do you— You know what, never mind."

I take off in that direction.

When I go in, I spot Jace right away, but I can't make myself move past the doorway. I can feel Zane right next to me, watching my every move. Jace is sitting toward the back, alone, with headphones on as he writes on a piece of paper. A few other students are grouped together, working on different projects while they talk about the upcoming prom—yet another thing I won't be able to do. Not that it matters. All of that seems so small compared to the fact that I won't be able to be with Jace, or my family. I look back at Jace, and I still can't make myself move any closer.

"He is fine," Zane says. "Well, maybe not fine, but he will be. He's tough," he says with a confidence that throws me off.

I feel the need to cry the moment it clicks. I look down at my sweater. This is how he knew this is my favorite. This is how he knew me. I sigh and look over at Zane.

"You were his guardian angel, weren't you?" I ask.

He gives me a short nod.

"What happened that night?" I whisper to myself, and I'm surprised when Zane actually says something.

"I wish I knew." He pauses. "Actually, I wish I was around to stop whatever happened." He looks over at me. "I'd have done everything in my power to save you if I'd been around."

As he says that, he sounds like a different person. I look into his green eyes, and I see the regret. He meant every word. I look back at Jace. Two of his friends are in this class, but they won't even look in his direction.

"He's not alone by choice," says Zane. "A lot of people blame him. Some say you two argued and you ran away from home. Some even think he is involved with your disappearance."

I gasp.

"But you know he didn't do anything," I say.

"I wasn't exactly around, but it doesn't matter what I know or think."

I laugh, and he gives me a funny look. "I don't get it," I say. "We never fought. Not even once."

"Yeah. I know," he snaps.

I walk over toward Jace's desk and sit on the one next to it, facing him. *He looks so sad,* I think to myself.

When I look up, I notice Zane looking over at the other side of the room, where I spot a tall and pale redhead staring at Jace. I know I've seen her before, but for the life of me, no pun intended, I can't remember her name. She has always been reserved—that is about all I can remember.

"Elsie Brooks," says Zane.

She goes back to reading her book, but every once in a while, she looks at Jace, and not with a simple *I'm into you* look.

I look from her to Zane. "She knows something."

CHAPTER 6

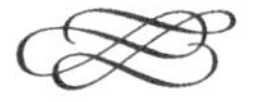

ZANE

I walk around the desk and stand in front of her, blocking her view of Jace.

"So what now?" I ask her.

She has this look in her eyes. I've seen that look many times before. She's plotting something, and I know her. Once she puts something in her head, she goes for it.

"Now, we follow her," she says, nodding toward the girl. She sighs and sits back, where she can see Jace again. "Do you miss watching over him?" she asks.

I just stare at her, not knowing how to answer that. The best part about watching over him was being around her. Well, that was the best and worst part all at once.

"How long were you his guardian for?" she asks when I don't say anything.

I shrug. "Two years—maybe less . . . " Since her fifteenth birthday almost two years ago. I remember the day like it was yesterday. They snuck out that night, and I had the glorious job of keeping them safe.

She sighs again, looking at him. "This is so unfair."

"Tell me about it," I mumble.

"What did you say?" she asks, looking at me.

"Nothing. Go on . . ."

She looks over at her ring and starts to play with it. She doesn't look back up for a while. She just sits there quietly, which kills me.

I close the distance between us, put my hand on her shoulder, and take us back to the library.

"What the hell?" she practically yells as soon as she realizes where we are. "What did you do that for?"

"That was enough for the day," I say.

She turns around, grabs a book, and throws it against the wall. A guy who appears to be in his thirties looks up from his book, rolls his eyes, and goes back to reading it like nothing happened. Sometimes, being in a town full of supernatural beings has its perks.

"Really?" I ask in a sarcastic tone. "This is exactly why I pulled you out of there. You were getting too emotional. I'm not dealing with a ghost who is throwing fits."

"Fine. Then don't," she snaps before she takes off—fast. And farther than she should be going.

"What are you doing?" I ask. She is mad. I know her. She won't stop until it's too late, and so I'm forced to follow. "Are you going to stop?"

"Nope!" She yells back.

"Do you even know where you are going?" I ask.

She doesn't say anything, but I keep following her until we reach her house.

She stops at the front door and looks back at me. She nervously bites her bottom lip.

"Do you want to go in?" I ask.

"I don't know," she says. I know her emotions are all over the place. I can feel it in ways that I shouldn't be able to. "I miss them." She pauses. "I need someone . . . familiar."

I nod toward the house, hoping that is enough to encourage her to do what she needs to do.

We go in.

It's almost noon, and we find her mom lying on her bed, sleeping. There is a bottle of sleeping pills next to her. Heidi just stands there, watching her.

"I'm going to step right outside of the room," I say. "Give you some privacy."

"Okay," she says, still staring at her mom.

"Heidi," I say, and she looks up at me. "Talk to her. That will help."

"It won't be the same."

"I know," I say, before I walk out of the room.

I don't know how much time passes before I finally go back in. I find Heidi lying down next to her mom, pouring her heart out about how much she misses just being able to hug her.

"I saw Jace today." She pauses and closes her eyes before she rolls onto her back. "It's so unfair to know that all of our plans are gone. We won't go to prom together, or college. We won't get married. I don't even know what I'm really doing here. I can't remember what happened to me, and there is this mystery thing I need to repair. I just want to find out what happened to me, so maybe you and dad will have closure." She looks back at her mom and sighs. "Sad thing is that the only one I can have an actual conversation with doesn't even want to be here."

If she only knew just how much I want to be here. To the point where sometimes I wonder if her being stuck here is all that bad. I let out a growl. I can't be doing this. I can't punish her by keeping her here for my sake.

I back out of the room and sit in the hallway until Heidi comes out and says she is ready to go.

It's already getting dark outside, but we quietly walk back to the library. Once we are on the second floor, Heidi walks over to the window and leans against it, watching people go by. And as much as I want to tell her there is no place I'd rather be, I know I can't.

~

HEIDI

I look outside and zone out.

"Heidi," I hear Zane say right behind me.

I turn around, and I find myself face to face with him. To my surprise, he pulls me into a hug, and it doesn't take long before I feel tears run down my cheeks as I bury my face against his chest.

"I'm sorry this happened to you," he says as he awkwardly continues to hug me.

After a while, he lets go and steps away. He walks over to a bookshelf, grabs a book, and sits down on the floor. I realize that I missed contact more than I thought I did. I walk over and ask if he minds if I sit with him. He nervously shakes his head. I don't think he is used to all of this . . . human stuff. I sit next to him and lean my head back against the wall.

"You were human before, right?"

He tilts his head to the side. "Yes, but I honestly don't even remember it anymore."

"I miss sleeping," I say. "And food. Oh my God. I miss food! Cheesy waffle fries and a juicy hamburger," I say, and we both laugh. I lean my head forward and look at him. "What would happen if I ate?" I ask, still laughing.

"Well, you have no digestive system so . . . I have no idea."

I laugh even harder and shake my head. I reach over toward a bookshelf, grab a book, and start reading it. After a while, I lean my head on Zane's shoulder. He tenses, but he doesn't say anything, so I stay where I am and keep reading.

CHAPTER 7

HEIDI

I'm surprised when Zane agrees to go back to the school without any attempts to talk me out of it or give me a lecture.

We go a little later in the day, and it's lunchtime, so he takes us straight to the cafeteria.

The first familiar face I see is Zoey Mills. I get distracted watching her interact with Miranda, Jordan Woods, and a few others. I'm happy to see that Zoey fit right in with everyone else.

I sigh and look past them.

It's not hard to spot the redheaded girl, and from there, it's not hard to find Jace. She's still doing that thing where she keeps looking at him from time to time.

Zane chuckles. "With that intensity, I'm surprised she doesn't feel that she's being watched."

I ignore what he said, hoping I'm not starting to pick up his habits. "I want to try something I read about in one of those books at the library," I tell Zane.

He gives me a puzzled look.

"What?" he asks, and he looks like he is afraid of the answer.

"I want to possess Elsie to talk to Jace." I can hardly believe those words just came out of my mouth.

"Nope. Not a chance."

I laugh. "I wasn't asking for permission. Look, I need to find out what happened. I can't think of any other way. So unless you have a better idea?"

"I'll come up with something," he says in a rushed tone.

"Well, I'm tired of just ghosting around. I need to do something!"

He rolls his eyes at me. "Fine. But I'm kicking you out of her body the moment I deem it necessary. Possessions can be . . . addicting."

"Fine," I say. At this point, I'll say whatever he wants to hear.

"Fine." He glares at me.

Once he agrees, I realize that I wouldn't have gone through with it otherwise. I feel nervous like never before. I begin to wonder how it is going to feel, or if anyone will notice. What if I mess up?

Zane watches me curiously. "If you're really going to insist on this, you probably shouldn't overthink it," he says. I just roll my eyes at him.

I wait until Elsie gets up to go to the bathroom, and I follow her in. Zane starts to come with me, but before he steps foot in the bathroom, I put my hand against his chest to stop him. Talk about awkward. The nervous look on his face is priceless.

"What?" he asks.

"Don't be a creeper. You're not going in the women's bathroom. I got this. I'm sure you'll know if I need help."

He looks down at my hand still on his chest, and that is when I pull away and go after Elsie.

I find her staring at the mirror. She is brushing her hair, trying to control how wild it is. I step behind her. Close my eyes. And then, hoping that this will work, I take a step forward. I can feel her body jerk, and her head leans back before leaning forward again. This feels horribly strange. I look in the mirror. I feel like myself, but I see her. I look down at my—well, *her*—arms and hands, and watch her fingers as I move them around.

I take a deep breath. Breathing . . . I never thought I would miss this feeling so much. I look in the mirror again and tilt my head to the side. I run my fingers through my—her hair. This feels so weird. Deciding that I need me—her to look more like me, I make a quick braid. I look in her purse to find eyeliner and lip gloss. I put it on and walk out of the bathroom.

Zane is right in front of the door when I open it. His eyes meet mine before he glances at the braid. "Was that necessary?" he asks.

My lips part to answer when his abrupt interruption startles me. "Don't talk to me. You don't want to sound—well, you don't want to make her sound like a crazy person, do you? Don't even look in my direction. I'll be with you. Let's go."

We go back to the cafeteria, where I spot Jace sitting alone. I slowly walk toward him, and I can feel her heart beating against her chest with every step I take. I'm standing right next to the table when I stumble back as the memories come in. From a large window at the Mills mansion, I can see Jace and me dancing. We are both laughing. When we stop, he reaches for my hand. He says something as I watch in horror, and then I run toward the woods. Jace stands there for minutes that feel like an eternity, before he runs after me.

I suddenly feel a jerk, and I find myself standing by Zane, with Elsie in front of me. She quickly sits in front of Jace and puts her head down.

"Are you okay?" Jace asks in a concerned tone as Zane asks me the same question.

I put my hand on Zane's arm in an attempt to steady myself as I watch their interaction in silence.

"I don't know," she says, looking confused.

Jace notices the braid. I can see it in his eyes when he remembers how I wore my hair back when it was longer.

"Here." He offers her his drink, before things go dark and I find myself back at the library with Zane.

"You have got to stop doing that!" I snap.

"What happened?" he asks.

"Can we go back?"

He shakes his head. "What happened, Heidi?" he asks in a soft tone.

I look up at him.

"I saw her memories of that night . . . Jace said something that upset me. I ran into the woods, and after a while, he ran after me."

Zane doesn't say anything at first. "You saw her memories?" he asks.

I nod. "It happened the other day at school too. When people walked through me, I saw glimpses of their memories of me."

He rubs his forehead, but doesn't say anything.

"You don't think he would—" he starts to say before I interrupt him.

"Of course not! How could you even think that? You probably know him as well as I do." I pause. "But I need to know more. Can I do what I did with Elsie by possessing him?"

I can see the look of horror in his eyes as soon as I say it.

"Absolutely not. This memory thing, as far as I know, is not even common for beings like you."

"Okay, whatever. It worked. Maybe it will work on him, and I'll know more."

"Don't bother," he says. "You try to possess him, and I'll pull you out before you even get that far."

I cross my arms over my chest, and he chuckles. "You're not going to convince me by acting like you're upset. Not this time."

ZANE

I can't let her get hurt. I don't care what answers possessing him will give her. Nothing good can come of it.

I can see her frustration in her every move—in her every word.

She stares me down, waiting for me to change my mind. She's so hardheaded, I guarantee she's already plotting the next time she'll possess the girl. I shake my head and I can't believe I'm about to suggest this.

"I have special abilities that I could put to good use. To help you," I say, against my better judgment.

She crosses her arms and stares at me. "Like what?" she asks in a doubtful tone.

"I can influence her so that she'll talk to him and ask anything you want to know."

Her jaw drops. "Really?"

I nod.

She watches me curiously and then says, "He's not just going to talk to someone he doesn't even know. Are you going to influence him to answer with the truth?"

I shake my head. "I can't do that."

"Why?" she asks, and I ignore it.

"He'll talk eventually. He's been alone for too long. People always need someone to confide in."

I know the moment I say that, I said all the wrong words. I can sense the jealousy radiating off her. She's not even a jealous person under normal circumstances, but I know that look. I felt that many times before, even though I shouldn't have.

"I don't like this, and—" she starts to say before I cut her off.

I throw my hands up in the air. She's infuriating sometimes. "We'll try my way. If you want it to stop, or if it doesn't work, sure, go ahead and possess him." I won't allow it to happen, but she can think that for now.

CHAPTER 8

HEIDI

I spend the next few hours looking out the window, trying not to drive myself crazy. That gets old quickly. I turn to find Zane sitting on the floor, reading a book. My attention goes straight to the couple on the cover, making me chuckle.

"What are you reading?" I ask, and he quickly closes the book and stuffs it in the row of books next to him. As mad as I was over the whole discussion about possessing Jace, I have to keep myself from laughing. The sight of an angel reading a romance novel is just amusing. He ignores my question, as usual, and I don't press it. This is not the time to piss him off. "I can't stay here all day. Can we go to the music store?"

He stands up and reaches for my arm, but I quickly pull away. "I'd rather walk there, if that's okay."

He gives me a short nod.

On the way there, I can't help but ask, "Do you read romance books often?" I grin. He actually looks embarrassed, so I go on. "Not that there is anything wrong with that. I just—I don't know. Are angels allowed to read that?"

"I'm not aware of any rules against it," he says in a dry tone.

"Oh, okay." I look away as we head toward the store, and I'm caught by surprise when he goes on.

"I read them to understand you."

I stop and look at him with confusion, wondering what the hell that means.

"Humans," he says awkwardly. "I read them to understand humans."

I shrug, and we continue to walk. "Is it helping?" I ask.

"Nope."

I chuckle. "I didn't think it would. You know . . . you can ask me questions," I say. "If there is anything you want to know. Anything at all."

He abruptly stops walking and looks at me. "What does it feel like to kiss someone?" he blurts out, and after the shock that he actually asked something passes, I grin and close my eyes for a split second. I then look down at the ring on my finger and sigh.

"It feels like magic," I say. "The more you kiss, the more you want to keep kissing."

I can feel myself blush. I look up at him, and he has this intense, serious look.

"Come on," he says, nodding toward the store.

We go in, and again, I welcome the familiarity of the place. I see Glenn saying goodbye to a customer. I go to the spot where we were before and sit on the floor. I lean my head against the wall, close my eyes, and enjoy the music, the smell, everything about this place.

I can hear Glenn's voice. "Hey. Where are you? I came in early today just to train you. Call me when you get this message."

"I'm here! Sorry I'm late." I quickly open my eyes and see Jace rushing toward the back. I glare at Zane because I know what's coming.

"Don't you dare!" I warn him. He doesn't look happy, but he doesn't try to get us out of here.

I stand up and walk toward Jace as he puts his books in the back of the store.

"You work here," I say with a smile on my face. He always loved music, and I'm glad he's doing something he loves.

I look over at Zane. He's still sitting on the floor, watching me like a hawk, but he stays put as I follow Jace around like some crazy ghost stalker, looking for any sign that he may be thinking about me, or missing me . . . anything. Not that it will make a difference. Deep inside, I know that will actually make me feel worse, because nothing can change the fact that I'm dead.

When things quiet down, Glenn says he needs to go make a call, and Jace sits down behind the counter and grabs a music magazine. I stand next to him, with my back against the counter.

I glance at Zane, and he quickly looks away, pretending that he's not watching my every move. I then look back at Jace.

"I miss you," I whisper, feeling stupid for saying something he can't ever hear.

Out of habit, I reach for his hand, and I freeze in place as I get hit with a flash of memory. It's dark, but I can see it clear as day. Jace stands somewhere surrounded by trees. There is snow on the ground. I look from the ground to his hand, and it feels like everything is happening in slow motion. He is holding my phone, and when he moves it, I see the blood—my blood—on his hand, and I can feel the guilt he feels. I gasp as I look into his eyes—this time, back at the music store. Maybe it is shock, but for a split second, I feel like Jace is looking right at me, and then, I'm back at the library.

"What happened?" Zane asks in a concerned tone.

Words don't come out. I stand here, staring at a blank space. I can't think. I can't.

I feel Zane's hands on each side of my face. "Heidi. Look at me. Heidi."

I look up at him. I feel numb. I—

"What happened, Heidi?" His gaze holds mine in a way that I can't look away.

I feel my hands tremble, and when I start speaking, I don't even sound like myself. "I think I was killed. And I think Jace may have done it."

Zane stares at me, and the silence becomes overwhelming. He's not denying it. He should be saying there is no way. He knows Jace, like I do—or like I thought I did. Every bit of me begs him to tell me I'm wrong. That it's insane that I even think that, but he doesn't say a word. He just pulls me into a hug.

"I don't understand," I say after a while.

"What makes you think he did that?" Zane finally asks.

I sigh and try to get the courage to say it out loud. "When I reached for his hand—I got a glimpse of a memory." I'm filled with horror once again as I tell him exactly what I saw.

"Maybe he just found your phone," he says, and I shake my head.

"I could feel his guilt, Zane. It was weird and overwhelming. Why else would he feel guilty?"

Zane gives me a confused look. "Could you feel what Elsie felt when you possessed her?"

I shake my head. "Just her memories."

"I don't understand how or why you can pick up on those things, but he wouldn't have hurt you, Heidi. We'll find out what happened, okay?" he says in a soft tone. He continues to talk to me, and I just nod in agreement, but at this point, I'm not even listening to him anymore. I can't get that image or that feeling out of my head.

CHAPTER 9

HEIDI

I keep replaying Jace's memory in my head over and over again. Zane knows it, too. He's sitting on the floor and doing a horrible job at pretending to read a book. I can tell that by the concerned look in his eyes and also by the fact that he won't stop staring at me. By midnight, I'm restless. I can't spend another second here. I need to go and do—something.

"I have an idea," he says as he gets up. He extends his hand, and I put mine in his. Next thing I know, we are standing in the middle of Serendipity Dance Studio, where I've taken ballet classes since I was four. I stand here and look around. The glass windows from floor to ceiling allow for the moonlight to come through, making the studio look even more stunning than usual.

"I missed this place," I say.

"I figured," he says. "But I wasn't sure if bringing you here would be a good thing or not."

"I'm not sure either," I say. "It sucks I will never be able to dance again."

"You could still dance," he says.

I walk over to the window and look outside. "It wouldn't be the same. I danced because I loved to dance, but there was also something special about people admiring what you are doing."

"I am here, and I can see you," he says in a soft tone.

I turn around and look at him. Those bright green eyes stare right at me. I wonder once again why he is being punished. Saying things like this don't sound very angel-like, especially with the way he looks at me, and right at this moment, I'm not sure that is a bad thing. A part of me feels different—human, maybe—at being noticed. Or maybe I'm just going insane because I have no interaction with anyone besides him.

He holds my gaze for a moment longer, before he says, "Do you want to leave?"

I nod. "But I don't want to go back to the library. I have an idea, actually. Can you take me to the Mills mansion?"

He tilts his head to the side, waiting for more.

All I say is, "To the ballroom."

He takes me straight there. I remember being in this room that night as if it was yesterday. I just wish I could remember the rest of the night.

I walk to the middle of the ballroom, stopping under the skylight. I get on the floor and lie down. Zane approaches me. He looks down at me with confusion in his eyes.

"This is something I've always wanted to do," I tell him, and he chuckles. To my surprise, he lies down next to me and looks up at the sky.

I sigh. "What is it like being an angel?"

"Not worth the sacrifices," he says in a bitter tone.

I look over at him. "You must've had to give up something really important to feel that upset about it."

He keeps looking up. "I wouldn't say give up. You can't give up someone—I mean, something you never had."

I look back up at the sky again, afraid to know more, because I have a feeling that this has something to do with me. I mean, the things he says, and he was Jace's guardian for years before this punishment. He even cared enough to know my favorite things. But I know that I can't stay here like this, feeling trapped.

"I'm afraid of what will happen to me when I move on . . . whatever that means. But I'm even more terrified of being stuck like I am now for eternity," I blurt out.

He turns his head to the side, facing me, and there is something different about the way he looks at me. "I wish I could promise you that everything will be okay, Heidi. I really do."

There he goes again. I let out a nervous laugh.

"Well, that sounds comforting," I say as he sits up, his back to me. *Ugh.* I have to know. "Zane?" I say, and he looks back at me. "I have to ask you something. It's more of a guess really. I just need to know," I start to babble.

"Go on."

"You know what it is that I need to repair, don't you?" I ask. He doesn't say anything, but I notice he tenses. "Your punishment and whatever it is that I need to repair are related, aren't they?"

I regret asking the moment I see tears in his eyes.

He looks away and lowers his head. "They are," he whispers. "But you don't have to worry about it. I'll make sure it's taken care of." He still avoids looking at me. "They're just trying to teach me a lesson. Make me realize there are consequences to everything I do, and that I should value what I am."

At this moment, my heart breaks for him. You can't force someone, angel or not, to do what their heart isn't into. And this also means there is a giant risk of me getting stuck here.

I can't even tell which one of us is made more uncomfortable by this conversation.

"Can we go back to the library?" I ask as I get up.

He doesn't hesitate.

~

Back at the library, I try to come up with something else to talk about, mostly to try to keep his mind off the conversation we just had. Unfortunately, my thoughts take me right back to Jace's memory, and then, something Zane said before about staying out at night pops in my head.

"What did you mean when you said that I wasn't ready for Havenwood Falls? I mean, I've lived here my whole life. I'm sure there is nothing I haven't seen."

He bursts into laughter.

"I'm glad you think that's funny." I keep staring at him, waiting on an answer.

"You should sit down," he says, making me feel uneasy. Just how bad can this be, considering everything else I've been going through?

He manages to stop laughing and sighs. "We're not the only ones around who are not human."

I relax. "Huh. I can't believe I didn't think of that before. So, there are other angels and ghosts. Why can't we go out there?"

He doesn't bother answering. I hate when he does that. He walks over to the bookshelf and picks up a book. I rush toward him and grab the book from his hand.

Looking up at him, I beg, "I need something to get my mind off Jace. Just please tell me. I don't care how shocking it is. Please, Zane."

He looks tense. "Sit down," he says.

I do. I sit on the floor of the quiet library, lit by nothing but the moonlight, and he sits in front of me.

"Do you remember the howls you heard on the night you awoke in the woods?"

I nod.

"Werewolves," he says.

I study his face, and he even looks serious. I burst into laughter. When I notice he's still not laughing with me, but just sitting there, watching my reaction, I stop.

"No way," I say.

He nods. "Vampires, shifters . . . you name it. Havenwood Falls is full of supernatural beings."

I give him a doubtful look.

"Everywhere you look. Everywhere you go. At school, I wouldn't be surprised if there are more supernatural beings than humans."

I grin at him. "Right," I say in a sarcastic tone. "Who? Give me names."

Zane scratches his chin and looks like he is deep in thought.

"Well," he finally says, "the Kasuns are wolf shifters. Julianna Fairchild comes from a long bloodline of fae, and Miranda—"

I burst into laughter, cutting him off. "You can stop. You're making this up, aren't you?"

He doesn't really give me an answer. He just shrugs and grins. He reaches for another book and hands it to me. "Read this. It will help keep your mind busy."

I slowly take the book from him and try to focus on reading it, which doesn't come easily.

When morning comes, Zane is ready to get us to the school, but I'm the one who doesn't want to go. I'm terrified. I'm afraid of seeing Jace. I'm afraid of finding out more.

CHAPTER 10

ZANE

It kills me to see how much that one memory she saw is hurting her. She spent the last few hours pretending to read the book I gave her, while I sat here, helpless and wondering what in the world I am doing telling her the things I told her last night, and most importantly, telling her that I will repair something that I'm not sure I want repaired at all. I hate that she's part of a higher plan to teach me a lesson—that I am the "thing" she needs to repair, which just makes me angrier at being what I am. And at Fate for putting her in my path. Several times a day, I have to convince myself that letting go and devoting myself to my destiny is what I should be doing, but I find myself wondering over and over again how bad it would be if she doesn't move on. I could walk away from it all. But then I remember her words. This is not what she wants.

When it's time to go back to the school, I can see how afraid she looks, but there is no way he did it.

"He didn't do it, Heidi. We'll find out what happened," I attempt to assure her.

I know she wants to believe me, but she can't. I can tell by how tense she is. She sighs and bites her bottom lip.

"Just say it. What's on your mind?" I ask.

"Let's say he just happened to find my phone. Why the guilt?" she asks.

"Well, if something he said is what led you into the woods, it's only reasonable for him to feel guilty."

She looks at the floor as if she's thinking it through. Then her eyes meet mine again.

"Are you ready to go?" I ask.

I know she isn't, but she nods. As I reach for her arm, she closes her eyes, and then we're at the school, in Jace's class.

At the sight of Jace, she takes a step back and just stares at him. She looks terrified. I'm scrambling to figure out what I should even say at this point, or if I should take her out of here, when I feel her hand slip into mine. Our fingers entwine, and now I'm scrambling for what to say again, but for other reasons.

"We could go," I finally say, but she shakes her head.

"I need to find out that it wasn't him. It couldn't have been."

When she tries to let go of my hand, I hold on to her, and surprisingly, she doesn't pull away.

"Come on," I say. "Let's walk around. We can come back during lunch, when I can get Elsie to actually talk to him."

She agrees and looks at him once again, before we go toward the hallway. Still hand in hand, we walk around, and I find her watching a group of students who are standing around, talking about prom.

"What is it?" I ask.

"What are they?" she asks, and I give her a confused look. "Vampires? Werewolves? Humans?"

I laugh.

"I didn't think you were serious," she says. "But nice attempt at keeping my mind busy."

I laugh again. "Come on," I say as I lead her to the cafeteria, where we wait.

It's not until then that I let go of her hand.

"Thank you," she says.

I raise an eyebrow at her.

"For the angelic support." She smiles, and I tense.

"I don't think holding your hand like that classifies as angelic support."

"Oh," she says. "Are you going to get in trouble for that?"

I shrug. "It doesn't matter. You needed me. I was there for you."

Embarrassed, she tilts her head down, avoiding my gaze, and I know I need to stop saying things like that. For my sake and hers. I have to remind myself that if she were to stay stuck here for eternity—that would be an eternity of her blaming me for it.

When she finally looks up, I'm the one who avoids eye contact.

"Can I ask you something?" she asks.

"Sure."

"Is it really that bad, being what you are?"

I shrug, and stop to think about it. "For me? Yes," I say, and she probably thinks I'm a jerk for not appreciating the privilege of being an angel. "It wasn't always like that. I was proud of being an angel at one point."

"What happened?" she asks.

"Fate," I say in a bitter tone, and I leave it at that. And to an extent, it's true.

If only I had never met her, things would've been so much less complicated. The strange thing is I don't even know why *her*—after a century—why she had this effect on me from the first time I laid eyes on her. Why I was so filled with jealousy the first time I saw her and Jace kissing. Why I fell for her more and more every day—when I saw her dancing, when I saw her laughing, when I saw her just being her. And the worst part is that the way I feel has rendered this punishment useless. Every day that passes, I care more for her, and every day, I'm further away from being saved.

When I get out of my own head and look at her, I see that she's nervous again. I start asking her questions about school to distract her, but avoiding things that would make her feel sad, like her plans for prom, become nearly impossible. Before we know it, we hear commotion as people come into the cafeteria.

I spot Jace right away, and Elsie not far behind. I'm a little surprised when I see Elsie sit down at the same table as him. I look over at Heidi, and she looks even more afraid now. Or maybe it's not fear, but something else.

"Did you do that?" she asks.

"What?"

"Influence her to sit with him?"

I ignore the question. More and more, I notice how much I've been doing this. I hate lying to her; yet, I feel this undeniable need to protect her.

"Come on," I say as I stand, and when she doesn't move, I extend my hand to her.

She puts her hand in mine and gets up. As I lead her toward them, I can tell how nervous she is by the way she's holding on to me. Once we're close enough to hear their conversation, I listen for the right moment to cut in. Elsie is telling him about one of the math assignments she needs help with when I see *him*—the one who gave my punishment.

I quickly let go of Heidi's hand. My hands turn into fists, and I can feel my fingernails digging into my skin as he watches Heidi and me. I didn't think they would be checking in like this. They rarely do, and I don't want Heidi anywhere near him.

Heidi seems too engrossed in Jace and Elsie's conversation to even notice.

I look at her.

"Heidi," I say, and she looks at me. The entire time, I'm trying to keep an eye on him to make sure he doesn't get any closer. I'm not sure if this is good or bad, but he just watches from a distance. Seeing the pain in her eyes, I hate having to do this even more. "Heidi, I need you to do something for me."

"What?" she asks in a tone that breaks me.

"I have to walk away for a little while. I need you to possess Elsie until I get back. As long as you are possessing her, you're safe here."

The pain in her eyes turns into fear.

"I'll be as close by as possible. But I need you to do this, Heidi. Please. And don't leave her until I am back. Can you do this for me?" I beg, and she nods.

"Promise no matter what you see or hear, you'll stay put until I get back."

"I promise," she says. I wait until Heidi slowly moves toward Elsie and possesses her before I walk away to meet the dominion angel.

CHAPTER 11

HEIDI

I stare at Jace and fight the urge to cry. He's going on and on about an assignment for class when I blurt out, "Do you miss her?"

I watch the blood drain from his face. He looks down at his food and leans back against his seat. His tone completely changes. "Of course I do."

We fall into silence, but not for long, mostly because I don't know how long we have. "I was at the Mills mansion that night. I saw her run into the woods. What happened?"

He looks up at me, and now he's the one who is on the verge of tears.

"Can we talk about something else?"

I just look at him, my eyes begging him to tell me more, even though I'm terrified of what that might entail. I absentmindedly pull her long red hair to the side and start to braid it. His gaze goes to my hands as I weave locks of my hair.

He sighs. "I can't talk about that night, okay?" he says as he pushes his tray away.

"Can't or won't?" I ask as I remove the rubber band from her wrist and put it around her hair.

"I can't." He leans forward and lowers his tone. "I heard the rumors. I didn't do it, if that's what you're getting at. Sheriff Kasun said I shouldn't discuss that night. That's all there is to it. And please don't ask me again," he begs.

I nod and leave it alone, knowing that I won't get anywhere without Zane's help. I look around for him, but he's nowhere to be found.

"She used to wear her hair like that," Jace says, pulling me back to the moment.

The way he says that raises goose bumps on Elsie's arm. "I'm sorry," I say.

He looks down at the table, avoiding my gaze. "Yeah. Me, too."

"Ask if he thinks you're still alive," I hear Zane next to me. I start to look his way when he stops me. "Don't. Keep looking at him," he orders.

I take a deep breath, and I notice how it doesn't feel the same anymore. Breathing has started to feel awkward.

"Do you think there is a chance she's still alive?" I ask, and he shakes his head. And that look of guilt is all over his face again.

"I wish that was the case more than anything else," he says, practically whispering. "But—" he starts to say. He then stops and just shakes his head, leaving me more confused than before.

"Maybe he'll talk more if outside of the school," says Zane.

I stare at Jace without saying anything. I start remembering the many times we were sitting here, making plans for after school. And now, I'm sitting here, across from the love of my life, wondering if he killed me.

Zane pulls me out of Elsie, but this time, I don't mind. I feel exhausted.

I see the look of confusion in her eyes before she asks, "Do you want to do something later today?"

And I know this is Zane's doing.

Jace raises an eyebrow at her.

"Come on," she says shyly. "What do you do besides school and work?"

"Nothing much," he says in a sad tone.

"Do you work today?"

He shakes his head, and I just stand here, feeling numb as I watch their interaction.

"How about the Burger Bar after school?" she asks, and he hesitates. "Just something to do. There's nothing to it. We'll go as friends. Maybe you can help me with my math homework."

He still hesitates, but finally agrees.

"I guess just meet me by my car after school," he says, and I feel the hint of jealousy creeping through. Maybe I don't need to know that bad—not if it's going to push someone new on him. And I know that's me being selfish, but I also know I can't handle seeing him with someone else.

When lunch is over, Zane and I stay in the empty cafeteria, and we sit where Jace and Elsie were.

"What's on your mind?" Zane asks.

He holds my gaze with those sad green eyes. I don't want to talk about it, but I find myself saying exactly what's on my mind.

"How much the thought of seeing him with someone else would hurt," I blurt out, and Zane gives me this sympathetic look, as if he can understand. Maybe those books are helping him remember human emotions after all.

"There is nothing going on between them," Zane says.

"Yet," I reply in a bitter tone.

Zane watches me with an intensity that makes me look away. "I don't think he could get over someone like you."

I'm caught by surprise, considering our conversation at the ballroom. Again, this doesn't seem like something an angel should be saying, and more and more, I start to believe that I will be stuck here forever, even if I do find out what happened to me.

I sigh. "I guess I can't expect him to be alone forever." His lips part to say something else, when I stop him. "Let's get out of here. Maybe we can walk around the school or something until it's time to go."

Zane gives me a wicked grin.

"What?" I ask in a suspicious tone.

"Come on," he says, and I follow him to the Spanish classroom.

"WHY ARE WE HERE?" I ask.

His grin grows wider. "To cheer you up."

"Ugh. I hated this class while I was alive. Why would it cheer me up now?"

He shrugs. "I know your teacher is not exactly a role model. He has said mean things to just about everyone in your class, and now, here we are. They can't see you. Let's say you wanted to play a few . . . hmmm . . . ghost pranks on him—no one would stop you," he chuckles.

I roll my eyes at him. "That's so immature. And again, are you sure you're an angel?" I laugh.

He raises an eyebrow at me. "Do you want to leave?"

I shake my head. "No!"

I can't believe I'm about to do this.

Zane takes a step back, and I stand here, looking at the teacher and students and pondering what I should do. After a while, I grin from ear to ear.

I look over at Zane and notice that he has been watching me with an intensity that makes me shy away.

"We need to make a quick stop by the art class," I say.

He follows me quietly as we go in. I grab a very small bottle of glitter glue, and then we go back. As Mr. Fernandez stands up to read something to the class, I walk over to his desk and put glitter glue all over his chair. When I look back at Zane, he's shaking his head and smiling. And when Mr. Fernandez finally sits down, after what's the longest lecture on earth, I'm laughing so hard it hurts.

"Sorry," I tell Zane. "I know this is stupid and immature, and—"

"You needed that laugh," he interrupts me. "It's good for the soul."

I smile at him. I then look back and watch as Mr. Fernandez stands up, and when he turns around, the entire class bursts into laughter. Even Brice Blackstone, who is shy and keeps to himself for the most part, can't stop laughing. It takes Mr. Fernandez a few minutes to figure out what's going on, which makes it even funnier.

"Well, I can't say that I'll miss this class." I look over at Zane. "Thank you," I say.

"My pleasure."

Zane takes me out of there before Mr. Fernandez can react. He says I would just feel bad later on if I had stayed, and I know he's right. I would never have done something like that when I was alive. We end up walking around the school until the last bell rings.

CHAPTER 12

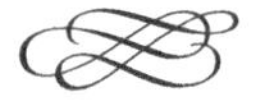

HEIDI

I freeze in place when I see Jace's dad's convertible. I close my eyes and relive the memories of that night as if it had just been yesterday. His dad's convertible parked on my street . . . the drive to the Mills mansion . . . the Christmas decorations on the way. Jace wouldn't let anyone but me ever ride in this car, because his dad would kill him otherwise. I can't let Elsie ride in the car with him. I go toward them, and Zane lightly wraps his hand around my wrist, holding me back.

I look at him, and I feel like my soul is crushed. "I can't let her in the car with him. It's too—personal. This means something."

"It's just a car, Heidi," says Zane. "And even if you possess her, that is still not you in the car with him."

"Thanks for the reminder," I snap.

"I didn't mean it like that, Heidi, but—"

"I know. I know. It's not your fault. It's the truth."

When I look back toward Jace, it's too late. They're already gone.

Zane gets us to the Burger Bar, and right next to the car. The top is down, and they are both laughing. Genuinely laughing, like they are having fun.

"So, I was thinking," says Elsie. "Were you planning on going to prom?"

"Keep your emotions under control," Zane warns, but I can't. *Music*, I think to myself as I hear the radio's static, and then my and Jace's song comes on. His smile turns into a frown, and before the food even gets there, he tells Elsie he needs to get home.

"This is about Heidi, isn't it?" Elsie asks, and he nods without looking at her.

"I'm sorry," she says.

He punches the steering wheel with both hands. And when he looks at her, there are tears in his eyes—and he breaks down, crushing me even more. "It was all my fault. Everything that went wrong that night was my fault."

Her eyes widen. "What do you mean?" she asks in a nervous tone.

Jace shakes his head. "Never mind. I need to get you home. Where do you live?" he asks.

I look over at Zane.

"Make him answer her!" I order Zane, and as usual, he doesn't acknowledge what I said. Instead, he gets close to Elsie, blocking my view, and the next thing I know, she's giving Jace her address.

"What did you do?" I ask.

"She doesn't need to remember what he just said," he says, before I turn around and stalk off toward my house.

Zane follows me from a distance.

The house is empty, and I go straight to my old room and lay down on my bed, burying my head under my pillow.

I can feel Zane in my room, but he doesn't say anything. I feel annoyed, irritated, and scared. Mostly scared.

When I finally look over, I see Zane sitting on the floor under my window.

"I still don't think it was him," he says.

I sit up on my bed, looking at Zane.

"You know what scares me the most?" I ask, and he shakes his head. "I don't understand how it could've possibly been him, and I hope you're right because, from where I sit right now, it doesn't look good. And yet, I don't love him any less—and that is what hurts the most."

ZANE

I sit here terrified, because I don't know how to fix this. I can't fix any of this, and now time is ticking. They want me to be here next to her, getting answers, and they want it to happen soon, or I will be reassigned again—and she will be stuck who knows where. Either way, I hate the thought of never being able to see her again.

I stand, go toward her bed, and sit near her. "Tell me everything you remember about that night—until right before the moment your memory fails you." I was there for that part, but maybe this will help with her memory.

She hesitates, then looks down at her ring. She looks so sad that I regret asking, but maybe what I'm planning will help. She doesn't look away from the ring as she tells me about them being outside the Mills mansion, how he put the headphones on her, playing her favorite song on his phone while they danced. That is all she can tell me without falling apart.

"Come with me?" I ask as I get up.

She rolls her eyes. "You keep asking that like I have a choice," she attempts to joke.

She gets up and just stands there. "Where are we going?" she asks. I don't answer. I just take us to the back of the Mills mansion.

It's already dark out, and she looks around, taking in our surroundings. "What are we doing here?" she asks in a sad tone.

"I want to try something to help you remember. If at any point you want me to stop, just tell me."

She nervously agrees.

"Close your eyes," I ask her. I close the distance between us, putting my hand on her lower back and pulling her against my body. She tenses and opens her eyes.

"I want to recreate the memory to see if it helps you remember," I explain, and she closes her eyes again.

She leans against me, and I start singing her favorite song, 'Leave a Light On' by Tom Walker, into her ear. She relaxes against me after a while, and we dance to almost the entire song before I stop and slowly pull away. Her eyes are still closed when I lean in and kiss her, just like Jace did that night—but that is not really why I kiss her. I've wanted to know what that would feel like from the moment I met her, and at this moment, knowing she will be pulled away from me soon, I know I would regret it for the rest of eternity if I didn't kiss her.

I ignore the burning pain on my wings as I savor every single move, every single second, of being this close to her. I don't stop until she pulls away. She looks at me, and I can see the confusion all over her face—or maybe it's shock. She just stares at me, taking me by surprise when she leans in and kisses me again. This time, her hand goes to the back of my neck, and I pull her even closer. Our kiss deepens, and we don't stop until she abruptly pulls away and spins around, facing the woods. I just stand here, watching her—knowing that I just made the biggest mistake. Yet I don't feel an ounce of regret.

CHAPTER 13

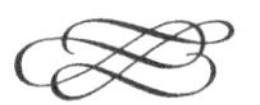

HEIDI

I run and I run, until I don't even feel the freezing cold anymore. It's not until after a while that I feel like someone is following me. I turn around and see the silhouette of a male figure.

"Jace?" I ask, scared.

He's not close enough, and at the sound of my voice, he stops where he is.

And the memory is gone.

I shake my head. I need to stop. I need to backtrack. The dance . . . the kiss . . . I need to remember what Jace told me. But nothing comes to mind. Nothing at all.

I look over at Zane, and he's just watching me, waiting for me to say something, and it's not until now that it hits me. "Are you going to be in trouble for kissing me?"

He shakes his head. "I had to—to recreate the memory," he lies.

I know this isn't true. I know he had been curious about kissing, and that felt like more. It wasn't a forced kiss to make me remember something. No one kisses like that without wanting to. And I should probably not have felt like I did when he kissed me, or when

I kissed him. Unless I just crave human interaction so damn much, and that is why I felt . . . something. I sigh. I can't think about that right now.

"I need you to take me to Jace's house," I say.

He raises an eyebrow.

"I was just so close to remembering. I remember running in the woods, and someone following me. Maybe I will remember more if I see him."

"It's late," says Zane. "Maybe tomorrow."

I shake my head. "I need to remember. Please," I beg.

Zane lowers his head and hesitates, but next thing I know, we're in Jace's room. He's sleeping. His window is open, and his TV is on, giving me just enough light to be able to see everything. I take a look around, seeing how everything is exactly the same. There are still pictures of us on his desk, and on his wall. I go toward the bed and reach for his hand, hoping to pick up a memory. I stay here for a while, with my hand on his, until he becomes agitated and then abruptly wakes up. I look at my ring, and I recall that he bought it from Summit Jewelry. I remember someone at school joking about some of their merchandise being special—in a magical sort of way. I chuckle. I guess anything is possible. I slowly slide it off my finger, feeling a little terrified of how he's going to respond to what I'm about to do—if it even works.

"What are you doing?" Zane asks in an alarmed tone.

"I need him to see this ring," I say, hoping that my plan will work.

Zane nods, but he looks like he's in a daze, just going along with whatever I say. "Make sure you are not in contact with the ring."

I drop the ring on top of Jace's cell phone, which is next to him. At the sound of the ring hitting the screen, he quickly turns his bedside lamp on, picks up the ring and stares at it as I put my hand over his again.

His memories come flooding in.

We dance until the song is over, and when he pulls away from our kiss, he takes my headphones out.

He is tense. I give him a nervous laugh.

"Are you going to tell me what's going on now?" I ask. "I have a really bad feeling about whatever this is."

He reaches for my hand, and pulls it to his lips.

He then takes a deep breath.

"I don't even know how to tell you this," he says. Through his memory, I see the fear in my eyes.

I try to pull my hand away, but he keeps a hold on me.

"Just tell me, Jace."

He looks down at my ring as he tells me, "My dad got another job." He pauses. "We're moving away from Havenwood Falls." He looks into my eyes and sees the blood drain from my face. "We're moving to Germany," he says. "And Dad thinks that a long-distance relationship is too much while I'm finishing school."

He watches as I panic. He agreed with his dad because he didn't see it working any other way. I pull my hand from his, and I run.

He watches me go. Not long goes by before he texts me. Minutes, maybe seconds pass. No reply comes, and he becomes agitated. He paces back and forth, looking toward the area where I went, before he takes off running after me.

"Heidi, if you're still here, please give me another sign. Please," Jace begs, pulling me away from his memory.

I look over at Zane.

"Not a chance," he growls.

I ignore him.

"I need my ring back," I say as I reach for it and grab it from Jace's hand.

Jace closes his eyes as I do, and I get hit by another memory. Jace in the woods—the ground covered in snow. He reaches toward the ground and picks up my phone. I feel his panic as he looks around, searching for me, and as he screams my name before he realizes he needs help. I see Jace handing my phone to Sheriff Kasun and telling him what happened as the guilt becomes unbearable. He blames himself, but only for not stopping me and for not going after me as soon as I took off.

The memory is gone, and Jace just sits there, staring at his hand. Zane goes toward Jace and touches his forehead—within seconds, Jace is lying down, sleeping, and Zane grabs the ring and puts it on my finger.

I look up at Zane.

"He doesn't need to remember this, Heidi. That will hurt him more than you will ever know," he explains.

I keep watching Jace sleep.

"What did you see?" Zane asks, and while looking at him, I take off my ring again and place it on the bed before I get up.

ZANE

She can't keep her eyes off him, even as she answers me.

"He was leaving Havenwood Falls," she says. "That is what he told me that night. His dad got a job in Germany, and they were moving. I was upset, so I ran." She looks at me then and smiles. "He didn't do it, Zane. It wasn't him," she says, and she looks so relieved.

"We need to go," I say in a rushed tone, before I take us to the library.

I feel overcome with anger. I rub my hand against my forehead as I pace back and forth.

I need to talk to the fool who sent me here, but I can't leave her.

"What's wrong?" she asks. Her mood has completely changed since we stepped foot back in the library. "Besides the fact that I died because I made the stupid decision to run into the woods. At night. In Havenwood Falls."

"Whatever happened to you wasn't your fault, Heidi," I say.

She looks down. "I made the choice—" she starts, but I interrupt.

"Look at me," I say. When she does, I can see the regret, and that just makes me angrier. "It. Wasn't. Your. Fault," I say again.

I leave out the part that I know this because it was my fault. The actions that led to her death were because of me, and I need to do something about it. That is the only way I'll be able to look at her again.

I clench my fists.

"I need you to possess Elsie again."

"What? Why?"

"I can't tell you that. But I need you to do this, and I don't know how long I'll be gone for."

For a split second, I see the terrified look in her eyes. "Where did you go at school when I had to possess her?" she asks curiously.

"I had business to take care of."

"Is that where you need to go now?" she asks, and I nod.

"Are you going to come back?"

"Of course," I say, but I can see the look of uncertainty in her eyes. It takes me by surprise when she closes the distance between us and pulls me into a hug.

"Please come back," she whispers. "I don't want to be stuck possessing her forever. If that's even possible."

I manage to relax. In times of need, she has this weird calming effect over me.

"That won't happen. I promise," I say, running my fingers through her shoulder-length hair.

It's the middle of the night when I take her to Elsie's house. Elsie is home alone and sleeping. Heidi possesses Elsie, and sits up on the bed.

"You'll be okay," I assure her before I leave.

CHAPTER 14

ZANE

Everything in me says I shouldn't get too far away from Heidi. So I go up to Elsie's rooftop and call out to him—to the dominion angel who punished me.

It doesn't take long before I hear him behind me.

"This had better be important," he says in an annoyed tone.

I turn around to face him, and there is an amused look in his eyes.

"All along . . . this was all because of me," I say, and he just crosses his arms over his chest and stands there with this attitude like he's better than the ones like me.

"Was all of this necessary?" I ask in a cold tone.

He raises an eyebrow, waiting to hear more, but by the grin on his face, he knows exactly what I am referring to. I could never understand how someone with his role can be so evil. Heidi didn't have to be put through this. They could've let her move on and punished me in other ways. He still watches me carefully, as if trying to assess what might be going through my head.

"You played with fate," he finally says. "You influenced the boy's family to decide to move, so that you could escape the burden of seeing her every day. I don't have to justify my actions when you are the one who started this mess. You've been breaking the rules ever since you met her, and it was about time someone noticed and handled your punishment."

I clench my hands into fists. "All I did was influence his family to move. She didn't have to die because of it!" I growl.

He shrugs. "Maybe she did. Maybe she didn't. You changed her path." He pauses and tilts his head to the side. "Did you really think that the boy moving and you not seeing her was going to keep you from feeling the way you do?"

"I don't—" I start to say before he interrupts me.

"Be careful. Angels shouldn't lie," he warns with a smirk on his face. "If it makes you feel any less guilty," he continues, "she didn't die that night."

"What do you mean?" I ask.

He chuckles. "The human girl didn't die until a few days ago. On the night when I brought her back and you were given your punishment."

"What happened to her?" I growl.

HEIDI

I lay here staring at the glowing plastic stars on Elsie's bedroom ceiling. Feeling restless, I decide to get up. I go to her computer and check on Jace's social media. She's already signed in. I click on his profile, and in a way, I get sad when I see he hasn't posted anything since I died. Well, besides post after post with my picture—asking people to share and to call if they recognize me. I start looking through our old pictures then—at town events, at school, at homecoming—and that's when I see Jace come up online. I nervously click on his name and send him a message.

Elsie: How come you didn't move?

It takes him a while to reply. I stare at the screen and feel my—Elsie's heart beat against her chest as I wait and wonder if he'll even bother replying.

Jace: How did you know?

Elsie: Small town . . . lol

Another long pause.

Jace: I begged my dad not to take the job. I said I wanted to be here, helping look for Heidi.

Elsie: And he stayed, just like that?

Yet another pause. This time, longer.

Jace: I was a mess. I don't think he felt like he had a choice. Look. I have to go, okay? See you at school.

And just like that, he's gone. I stare blankly at the screen for a while. When I feel like I can't take it anymore, I close the window and stare at the desktop picture with my mouth hanging open—a picture of Jace and Elsie. Only, it's not really her. She just edited her face over mine. I feel sick to my stomach. I shut off the computer and turn the light on to find there are more pictures on her wall—my pictures with Jace, replaced with her and Jace.

I can't stand to be in her body a second longer. I have no idea where Zane is, but hoping that he is at the library, I rush out the door.

I barely get across the street when I hear Zane's voice.

"Heidi!" he yells.

I stop and turn around. I look everywhere, but I'm unable to find him. Next thing I know, he's standing in the middle of the street, in front of me—well, in front of Elsie. I'm about to leave her body when I lay eyes on the guy behind Zane, and Elsie's memories come crashing in.

Elsie when she was about seven years old, playing with a boy twice her age. Elsie a few years later, crying over him after a motorcycle accident took his life and almost took hers too. And him coming to Elsie, his little sister, in what seems like a dream. He sits on her bed at night, watching over her as she sleeps. He promises her that he'll make her every wish come true. He says that he hates seeing her alone, and that if Jace is who she wants, he's going to make it happen.

Her memory morphs into mine. I'm running and running, crying over Jace's news, when I hear something. I stop, turn around, and see the silhouette of a guy about Jace's height.

"Jace?" I ask nervously. I want it to be him, but deep inside, I know it's not. He disappears. I frantically look around, and when I start to run back toward what I hope is the right direction to the Mills mansion, I feel something hit my head. Hard. Before my eyes close, I see him—the same guy who stands behind Zane right now.

CHAPTER 15

HEIDI

I don't remember leaving Elsie's body, but when I'm back to the here and now, I'm no longer in the middle of the street. I'm back at the library, sitting on a chair. Zane is kneeling in front of me, his eyes full of concern.

I sit here, in a state of shock, and it takes me longer than it should to notice that his wings are out. Beautiful, pure white wings that clash with his dark hair and green eyes in the most perfect way. He is breathtaking, and for a while, looking at him allows me to escape my reality. I'm completely mesmerized by him, and it's not until his wings vanish in front of me that I look into his eyes.

"I'm sorry," he says, and for a split second, I wonder why he is apologizing.

I slowly lean forward. "I remember everything, Zane. The guy that was with you—how do you know him?"

"He's an angel. One of the ones in charge. He gave me this assignment."

I'm so angry. I practically jump out of the chair and get as far away from him as possible.

"Please tell me you are lying," I demand. I know Zane is good, but I also know he doesn't care for being what he is. "Angels are supposed to be good," I say—more to myself than anything else.

I look at Zane and meet his curious and concerned gaze. "He killed me, Zane."

I can see the shock in his expression. Or maybe it's disbelief. So I go on and tell him about the memories. About how he's Elsie's brother who died in a motorcycle crash. The promises he made her and her infatuation with Jace.

Zane stands in the middle of the room, looking terrified. "This can't be true. A dominion angel wouldn't even be this young and definitely no . . . no!" he growls. "This is impossible," he says as he frantically starts to pace back and forth. "I have to talk to him."

I stand here, staring at him. I shake my head. "Then I'm going with you, because I'm not possessing her again."

We end up staying, but Zane calls out to the angel once . . . twice . . . when he calls out to him again and nothing happens, Zane loses it. In a blur of movements, he turns around and punches the wall with such strength that the bookshelves near him vibrate. Finally, he sits on the floor underneath the window and buries his face in his hands.

I sit next to him and wait until he looks up before I ask, "Is it possible that he isn't one of you?"

Zane just sits there, staring at the other side of the room as if he's in a daze.

"Zane?" I say in a low tone.

He doesn't say anything in return, but he does look at me with those sad green eyes.

"I don't get why he would put you through this punishment if he's the one who killed me," I say before I fall into silence and just sit here, with Zane looking at me in the most pitiful way.

ZANE

I can't even begin to understand how any of this happened. I slip my hand into hers and sit with my head leaning back against the wall, knowing that these are the last few moments we'll have together. She knows what happened to her, and there is no fixing me, but I can't leave her stuck here. When the sun rises, I'm going to tell her the one thing that's going to make her hate me forever—that I'm responsible for what happened to her. And then I'm going to call another Dominion to report Bryson before he comes near her ever again, beg for forgiveness, and do whatever I need to do so Heidi can rest in peace.

After a while of sitting in silence, Heidi leans her head against my shoulder. "And I thought humans were complicated," she says.

I chuckle. "Some of us were human before."

She looks up at me. "I don't know what's going to happen to me, and I'm guessing neither do you, but I need you to promise me that you're going to try to be Jace's guardian angel again. Someone needs to keep him away from Elsie."

I close my eyes and lean my head back against the wall. I want to tell her the truth about why I'm no longer his guardian, but I can't—even though she probably suspects it.

We spend the next few hours here, just sitting, and when the sun rises, before I can even call another angel—any other angel—she says, "Can you take me to see Jace? Even if it's the last time."

I nod and take her to his house. He's still sleeping. She sits on his bed, and I tell her I'll be right outside of the room. I watch her watching him. She doesn't take her eyes off him for one second. When I close the door behind me, there is an angel already waiting. I remember seeing her once before. She's one of the older ones.

"It looks like we have a mess on our hands," she says.

"How did any of this happen?" I ask in a frustrated tone.

"We weren't monitoring you, Zane. I'm ashamed to say that Havenwood Falls keeps us busier than we'd like, and you've always done the right thing or had the best intentions in mind. Even when doing something questionable, like influencing Jace's family to decide to move, you were trying to do the right thing. You can't blame yourself, Zane. Yes, you changed her path, but her life didn't end because of that. Bryson Brooks pretended to be a Dominion. His actions killed her—not your decisions."

"You already knew? For how long?" I ask.

"It's recent. Bryson was bragging to another about what he was doing to you. We believe it was done out of jealousy. Bryson told him about that night and about how he," she looks down for a split second, "played you." She pauses. "The angel he talked to came forward."

I can't even face her, but I know that I have to. I look up and meet her eyes with every intention of asking to see him. Before I even ask, she says, "He ran off. We have been unable to find him."

I clench my fists. "I don't want another assignment after this, unless it is to help locate him," I say, and she nods.

"What about Heidi? What happens to her now? What happened to her all along?"

She leans against the wall. "She was in a coma. She was kept right outside of Havenwood Falls so she wouldn't be found. Bryson wasn't sure what to do with her, so he basically just kept her in that state until she died."

My eyes fill with tears. "Where was her guardian angel? I've never even seen—"

She shakes her head, looking down toward the floor.

"Bryson?" I ask, and she nods. "He was the one. Only, he was never around Heidi much, and we didn't have reason to know that, because she was always protected." Of course she was always protected. I was always around. "He asked to watch over her around the same time you came along. I'm sorry, Zane."

She hands me a piece of paper. "She was buried at this address. Take Heidi there. That's all you need to do. She is at peace. She'll move on once you get there."

I nod once before I turn around and walk into Jace's room.

Heidi is standing there, still watching him, and when she hears me, she turns around and crashes into my arms. The pain I feel from seeing her like this is more than enough punishment for my part in all that happened.

I kiss the top of her head.

"Are you ready?" I ask when she finally seems to calm down.

She pulls away and walks over to Jace once more. She glances over at his table, and I see her ring there. She looks at him one last time before she walks back toward me.

I extend my hand, and Heidi slips her hand into mine.

I decide not to tell her about her guardian. She doesn't need any more reasons to hate my kind. But once we're out of Jace's room, I stop her.

"I was able to talk to another angel." I feel my hands tremble as I tell her what happened. "You didn't die until that night you awoke in the woods. You were in a coma under Elsie's brother's care. He was hiding you." She listens. She just listens without saying one word and without reacting at all. "I was given the address where you were buried."

"Where is he now?" she asks.

I sigh. "He is missing, but he won't be for long. I'm going to find him. He'll be punished for what he did to you. This I promise you."

Heidi looks at me, and I can't quite read her. Maybe she just feels as numb as I do. I look down, because this is not something I want to do. The thought of being without her presence is unimaginable, but I know how selfish it would be for me to keep her here for my sake. The thought of her having to endure watching lives go by as Jace moves on and her parents grow old, and not being a part of that, gives me the strength to do what I need to do. I close my eyes for a split second and wait a moment longer before I say, "Once I take you there, you'll move on. You'll be at peace."

She sighs, and after a moment of silence, she says, "I hate to keep asking for favors, but can you take me to see my mom and dad before we go?"

"For you, anything," I tell her before I take her to her house.

Her parents are in the kitchen, quietly eating their meal.

She watches them with a smile on her face. "I got so lucky to have them as parents," she says before looking at me. "That thing that you do with influencing people," she says, and I freeze. I have come to hate the reminder that I can do that. She bites her bottom lip and looks down toward the floor before she looks up at me again. "I don't want them to be alone, Zane. Can you make them—I don't know . . . maybe foster kids or something."

"Of course."

"You won't get in trouble for that, will you?" she asks in a concerned tone.

"I won't," I assure her. I would do this whether trouble was a consequence or not.

She looks at them once more before she closes her eyes.

"I'm ready," she says, but instead of taking my hand, she walks out of the house. On the front porch, she stops and looks back at me. "Once we get there, how fast am I going to be gone?"

"I honestly don't know," I tell her.

She gives me a sad smile and closes the distance between us.

"In that case," she says as she inches forward and gives me a kiss on the cheek, "thank you, for everything, Zane." She pulls away. "And so you know, because I know you were curious about it . . . that kiss was not bad at all."

She winks, and I'm the one looking away now.

CHAPTER 16

ZANE

Everything happens so fast. The address I was given is outside of Havenwood Falls and in a secluded area. I can feel the energy shift the moment we get to the exact spot where she was buried, and just like that, she's gone before I can say another word. She just vanishes in front of my eyes, and I feel the hole in my soul the moment that happens.

I stare at the dirt on the ground for what feels like an eternity. She's at peace now. This is how things work—only, this is not how things should've been for her. I know I need to leave, but I can't. I can't leave her here. What I am . . . my purpose . . . none of it matters as much as she does. I remember hearing a story decades ago, of an angel who did the unimaginable, but maybe it's only considered unimaginable because no one else has tried it.

I start digging, and I keep digging until I see the white sheet. I don't open it. I just cradle her in my arms, close my eyes, and focus on healing her—not for me, but for her. She should get to have the life she dreamed of—even if that means being with Jace. And as much as I'm filled with doubt that this will work, I know that I have to try. Her soul only moved on a few minutes ago. Maybe, just maybe, there is a chance. After a while, I feel weak, and I'm about to quit trying when I feel movement.

I carefully unwrap her then. Her eyes are still closed, but I can see the color slowly returning to her face. The cut on her forehead takes me back to the night when she awoke. I let my wings out as I cradle her—bringing her closer to my chest. I hold her for a while longer, just listening to her faint heartbeat and shallow breathing, before I take her to the Havenwood Falls Medical Center. I make sure there is no one around before I go up the steps and slowly put her down on the ground, next to the front door. I knock on the door, make myself unseen, and wait. A doctor with salt-and-pepper hair and blue eyes—Jasper Underwood—comes to the door and rushes toward Heidi. He picks her up as he calls for help. I follow them in, even though I know who he is, and I know he'll heal her.

He carries Heidi to the exam room and lays her down on the bed. He asks one of the nurses to get everything ready for lab work, and when she steps out, he looks in my direction. I know that since he's fae, he would've sensed me here.

I put my wings away. I don't even know why I do it, other than my knowledge that I've made far too many mistakes to be considered an angel. Not that I feel an ounce of regret. I'd have traded anything, my soul included, just to have her around again.

I make myself visible.

He gives me a curious look, and I wonder if he is trying to figure out what I am. I don't bother answering.

"She looks familiar," he says. "Who is she? What happened?"

"That is Heidi Bennett. She went missing on the night of the Cold Moon Ball. I don't know much of what happened," I lie—this angel thing is obviously not right for me anymore. He knows I lied too, but he pretends he doesn't. I suspect he's used to not asking too many questions around here.

"Did you find her?" he asks, and I nod.

"Outside of town. I brought her straight here." I pause. "I assume you'll ask the nurse to call her parents," I say. "If you can, ask them to call Jace Edwards too. She'll want him here when she wakes up," I say before I make myself unseen again.

He heals her more than what I had already done. I watch her sleeping peacefully as he tells Rachel Freeman, a nurse with dirty-blond hair and blue eyes, to call the Bennetts and Jace Edwards. The nurse gives him a puzzled look when he says Jace's name, and then her eyes widen the moment she realizes who Heidi is.

"Don't call Sheriff Kasun yet," he warns her. "Let her family see her first without all the commotion. It's not like he'll be able to question her right now anyway."

The nurse nods and quickly leaves the room.

Minutes go by before her parents, Jace, and his mom rush into the medical center, and then to the room, guided by Jasper Underwood. Her mom and dad both cry on one side, and Jace holds on to her hand on the other side of the bed. After a moment of watching her, he pulls her ring out of his pocket and puts it on her finger. I approach her from Jace's side, ignoring the fact that I feel consumed by jealousy, and when I brush my finger against her forehead, she wakes up.

She slowly opens her eyes. "Jace?" she says.

By now, he's crying too. I take a few steps back as he leans down and kisses her.

"How are you feeling?" he asks.

I stand here, leaning against the wall with my eyes on her. I know this was the right thing to do, but it's weird seeing her human again.

"I don't know," she says.

The nurse asks everyone to step outside for a little while to do some lab work, but I suspect she does that to keep Heidi from being too overwhelmed.

When everyone steps out, the nurse looks at Heidi. "Try to get some sleep. They'll all be here, but you need to rest," she says.

Heidi nods and closes her eyes. When the door shuts, Heidi opens her eyes again and looks in my direction. For a split second, I feel like she's looking right at me. I chuckle, knowing how stupid that sounds.

While still looking in my direction, she grins in a way that's not quite like her.

"Hi, Zane. Miss me?"

I freeze in place. She chuckles as she slowly gets up, pulling the IV out of her arm. While I can't move at all.

She approaches me, without taking her eyes away from mine. She stops when she is inches away from me and rests her hand against my chest.

"What are you doing?" I ask.

She grins. "I assume there is no saving you anymore, so . . ." Her grin widens. She leans in and kisses me.

READ MORE ABOUT HEIDI, Zane, and Jace in *Blurred Lines,* coming May 2019.

We hope you enjoyed this story in the Havenwood Falls High series of novellas featuring a variety of supernatural creatures. The series is a collaborative effort by multiple authors. Each book is generally a stand-alone, so you can read them in any order, although some authors will be writing sequels to their own stories. Please be aware when you choose your next read.

Other books in the Young Adult Havenwood Falls High series:

Written in the Stars by Kallie Ross
Reawakened by Morgan Wylie

The Fall by Kristen Yard
Somewhere Within by Amy Hale
Awaken the Soul by Michele G. Miller
Bound by Shadows by Cameo Renae
Inamorata by Randi Cooley Wilson
Fata Morgana by E.J. Fechenda
Forever Emeline by Katie M. John
Reclamation by AnnaLisa Grant
Avenoir by Daniele Lanzarotta
Avenge the Heart by Michele G. Miller
Curse the Night by R.K. Ryals (August 2018)
Blood & Iron by Amy Hale (September 2018)

More books releasing on a monthly basis.

Stay up to date at www.HavenwoodFalls.com

Subscribe to our reader group and receive free and exclusive stories and more!

ABOUT THE AUTHOR

Daniele Lanzarotta is the author of young adult and new adult paranormal/fantasy/contemporary novels, including the Academy of the Fallen Series, the Sudden Hope novels, and A Mermaid's Curse Trilogy.

Daniele is also a filmmaker and CEO & Founder of Elysian Nightfall Studios. She has recently worked on Virginia-based short films as the Second Assistant Director and Still Photographer. Daniele is currently working on the development stage for the adaptation of her novel, Sudden Hope, which she also plans to film in VA. She is also working on other film and writing projects.

She enjoys watching hockey, playing Rock Band, Guitar Hero, and spending time with her husband, two daughters, and the family dog.

Website: www.danilanzarotta.com
Facebook: www.facebook.com/danilanzarotta
Twitter: www.twitter.com/danilanzarotta
Instagram: www.instagram.com/danilanzarotta

ACKNOWLEDGMENTS

I knew from the beginning that writing Avenoir was going to be a different experience. And it was. It was different, challenging, and so much more! I quickly fell in love with Havenwood Falls and its characters. And I'm grateful to everyone who supported me along the way.

Thank you to Jocqueline Protho for introducing me to the Havenwood Falls world, and opening the door to this amazing opportunity.

Thank you to the readers. One of the many cool things about this project is that you got to know a little about Heidi even before my official first draft was done. Your enthusiasm and passion for the series made this writing journey extra special.

To the Havenwood Falls authors, it has been so much fun to collaborate with you. Thank you for answering questions and helping me find my way around Havenwood Falls and its residents. I'm lucky to be part of such an amazing group of authors.

Finally, I want to thank Kristie Cook for creating such an amazing world and for allowing me to be part of it. I learned so much from this experience. I can't begin to tell you how impressed I am by everything that you do, and I look forward to seeing Havenwood Falls grow more and more.

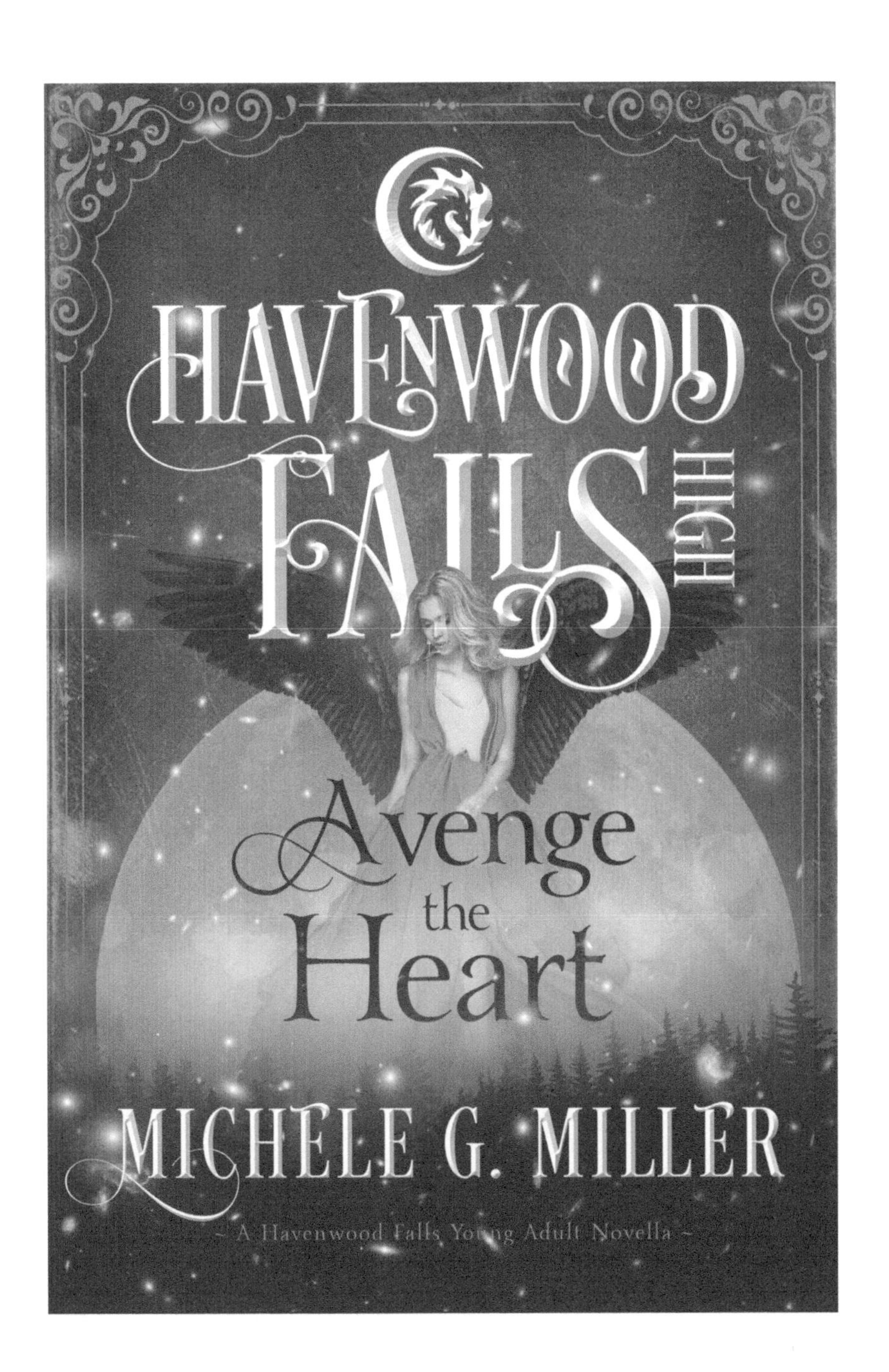
HAVENWOOD FALLS HIGH
Avenge the Heart
MICHELE G. MILLER
~ A Havenwood Falls Young Adult Novella ~

Avenge the Heart (A Havenwood Falls High Novella) by Michele G. Miller

Nearly dying, being stalked by a reaper, and finding her soulmate, all before Christmas, were not items on Vivienne Freeman's senior year bucket list. Now that Vivienne's survived December, Breckin Roberts decides they've had enough excitement for one year. As January rolls around, he is determined they will finish out their school year like normal teens. Except there's nothing normal about these two.

When Vivienne's supernatural abilities manifest, Breckin questions whether the changes are due to their soul bond, his healing her, or something more. They turn to Elias for answers, only to discover there's an entire history connecting their families they knew nothing about.

As the fallen descend on Havenwood Falls, Vivienne and Breckin are caught in a fight bigger than themselves. They must unravel the secrets and avenge the heart before any chance of redemption is lost forever.

AVENGE THE HEART

AN EXCERPT

"Why are you so glowy?" Zara asks in her faux British accent as she drops her ice skates on the wooden floor and lowers herself into the vacant seat across from me at Coffee Haven.

"Well, hello to you, too."

"Oh my gosh! You're pregnant!"

I choke. Thank God I hadn't taken a drink of my coffee. "What?"

"You are radiant, Viv. Like ridiculously so."

Careful not to crush the paper cup in my hand, I lean across the table and look my best friend in the eyes. "So, I'm pregnant?"

"Well, you are with Breckin . . ."

"And?" I bite the inside of my cheek.

"He's hot, and Breckin Roberts. And you're together twenty-four seven."

"My boyfriend is hot, so logically speaking, I'm pregnant." I return to my casual position. "It's happened—you've finally gone mad."

Zara's dark eyes study me intently. How much could I have

changed since last night? I kick her shin. "Stop dissecting me. I'm not pregnant."

Her freshly manicured red nail taps her chin. "Are you positive?"

"Yes, I'm positive," I hiss. "You have to have sex to get pregnant. I'm not having sex, Z. Plus, we've been together for three weeks. I might lose my mind around him, but I still have my morals. Give me some credit."

Her slim shoulders lift. "You're right, sorry. But seriously, you're—"

"Glowing," I interject and tug at the neck of my sweater. "I got it."

"Very well, backing off." She unwraps the frilly lace-edged scarf from her neck and looks beyond me toward the menu hanging above the counter. "I'm going to get a hot tea." Her eyes remain firmly set on my face until she's at my back.

Paranoia sets in. *Glowing?* I look at my hands, searching for the glow she speaks of. Nothing. I gaze around Coffee Haven, and no one stares back. The manager, George, chats up Zara as she orders. The gossip ladies are in their usual spot, getting their last batch of gossip in for the year over coffee and scones. Things are normal, for Havenwood Falls, anyway.

"So, where is lover boy? Is he not coming?" Zara asks when she returns to the seat across from me.

"To ice skate at the park? Do you know Breckin at all?"

Her booted foot nudges mine. "Evidently better than you do."

I look up, and there's Breckin, walking by the large picture window and entering the shop. He's dressed in his usual black, a slouchy beanie on his head, and the striped scarf I bought him for Christmas hangs loosely around his neck. He doesn't need those things: hats, scarves, gloves. He doesn't need the jacket or hoodie either. My angel stays warm all on his own, but keeping up appearances when you're a supernatural being is a priority.

His amber-flecked eyes catch mine the moment he's inside, and my stomach flips. He has that power over me. His name alone shoots tingles through my body. The sight of him lights up every nerve ending I own and tightens my core. Maybe I am pregnant. If anyone could get a girl pregnant merely by looking at her, it would be Breckin.

Zara draws a sharp breath. "Viv, you're flickering like those defective tree lights at Napoli's." She touches my hand, and the room turns sideways. "Viv?"

Everything goes fuzzy, and my head becomes too heavy to hold up.

"Vivie?" Breckin's breath grazes my ear, his pine-and-snow scent bringing things back into focus. "Hey, are you okay?"

I blink. *What the heck happened?* I'm sitting at Coffee Haven, leaning heavily against a kneeling Breckin, while Zara clutches my hand like a vise. "Did I pass out?"

Breckin's warm hand cups my cheek. "Only for a moment. I walked in and you, well, you just kinda fell forward. I caught you before the table could give you a concussion."

"I fell forward?"

"Are you sure you're feeling okay? That was bloody freaky, Viv. You were—"

"Pale," Breckin interrupts. He reaches across the table and grips Zara's wrist where she still holds my hand. "Viv hasn't eaten today, and had a little sugar crash. She's fine, but maybe you should get her a muffin."

My jaw drops. He's using compulsion.

Zara's dark eyes flare, before Breckin releases her and she stands. "Let me get you a muffin. You should have eaten this morning."

"Chocolate chip," Breckin calls over his shoulder.

"I'm her best friend, Breckin Roberts. I think I know her favorite muffin."

His mouth twists in a subtle smile as he stands and drags Zara's now empty chair closer. "You all right?" he asks, pressing his lips to mine in a chaste kiss that leaves me wanting more.

"I'm fine." I take inventory of my body. Other than the pouting my mouth does at his leaving mine so quickly, everything seems normal. My heart beats, my pulse is steady, my vision is clear, my head pain-free. "The room just sort of flipped on me. I don't know."

I'm back at his side, cuddling into his warmth. *When did I move toward him? What the heck? Crap, I'm practically sitting in his lap. In the coffee shop.* I right myself. The gossip crew will have a field day with our display. Sure enough, Irene Beckett and Laverne and Sybil Carson watch with narrowed eyes.

Breckin squeezes my shoulder. "Have you felt okay this morning? Last night?"

"I'm fine," I say, more firmly this time. "What are you doing here, anyway? Yesterday you said it would be a cold day in hell before you spent an afternoon ice skating with a bunch of people in Danzan Park."

His brows raise, probably at my ornery tone. "I changed my mind."

"Why?"

Zara thrusts a sugar-topped muffin in my face, cutting off his reply. "One muffin."

"Thanks, Z," I say, taking the muffin from her hand. I'm not hungry, but who can resist the smell of a freshly baked chocolate chip muffin? I tear the edge off the top and pop it into my mouth. *Thank you, sweet creator of chocolate. So good.*

"Are we going, or what?" Zara picks up her skates. *I guess that's all the time my best friend plans on giving me to recuperate.*

I open my mouth with every intention of backing out, but Breckin beats me to the punch. "Yep, let's go." He stands and grips the back of my chair.

Evidently he's not worried about whatever happened to me when he walked in either. Or he's putting on a show for the benefit of onlookers, and Zara.

"You don't have to come with us, Breckin," I tell him, not for the first time since Zara and I planned this outing a few days ago. He's not big on public spectacles, which is a hard thing to avoid when you live in Havenwood Falls. He's humored me this break with all the town traditions he's allowed me to drag him to.

"Yeah, he does." Zara pins him with her gaze and crosses her arms over her chest. "If you keep finding ways to bail on hanging out with me, Breckin, I'm going to take it personally." A delicately plucked brow curves up, challenging him.

Breckin snorts. "Zara, if I didn't like you, you would know."

She swings her gaze to me. "See, this is why I like him. I like your honesty, Roberts. Let's go take advantage of the December sunshine and have some fun."

Breckin pulls my chair back, picking up my coffee cup as he does. He moves close as I stand and throw the oversized bag carrying my skates over my shoulder. "I told you I wanted you to have normal, remember? If this is your normal, then I'll enjoy it for you."

Like the square, Danzan Park is full of families enjoying the last day of the year and the sunny winter afternoon. Zara and I have skated at the lake during Christmas break since we were little. It's tradition. When we were too young to come alone, our mothers packed hot chocolate and snacks, and froze their buns off for hours while we twirled around the ice. We liked pretending we were Olympic figure skaters, on our way to golden glory. It didn't matter that neither of us showed much promise; it was fun. It still is.

"I bet I can still spin faster than you," I taunt Zara.

She laughs and glides her way back, stopping next to Breckin, who isn't wearing skates, but is instead standing on the ice in his boots.

"No way. I was always faster," she tells my smirking boyfriend.

"In your dreams. Watch." I skate a small circle and pull my arms and one leg into my body, forcing a spin. The air whistles past my ears. Zara and Breckin's faces whirl by as my revolutions speed up. Around and around, her dark skin, his dark clothing. White snowcapped mountains, then other skaters. The scenery is a blur as I rotate faster and faster.

"Viv, if you break something, I'm gonna laugh." Zara teases, but there's an undercurrent of worry in her words.

Breckin tells me I need to slow down. I scoff. "I do not need to slow down." He growls. "Fine, I'll stop."

I force my arms away from the center of gravity, breaking the aerodynamics and slowing my spin down. Jutting out my foot, I stick my toe pick into the ice with a smile. Then I curtsy, sinking low and lifting my head to three very different faces.

Zara's olive complexion is pale, her mouth wide, her expression confused.

Breckin bites his lip and crosses one arm over his waist. He rubs at his jaw thoughtfully.

The third face I do not recognize, but his eyes cut through me like laser beams. He's beyond the frozen lake, among a crowd of people out enjoying the winter sun. His height and chiseled good looks make him stand out. I study him, my senses on high alert. *He doesn't belong here*. He's dressed for a fashion show—in a camel jacket and turtleneck sweater that look like they were tailored for his wide frame—not a day of fun in the park. *Who is he?*

Breckin touches my arm, and my attention snaps from the unknown man. "Are you dizzy? Because watching you spin like that made *me* dizzy," Breckin jokes, his fingers finding mine.

"You?" I ask. *The angel who flies like he has a death wish?* He chuckles under his breath, and I meet his handsome face with a smile. Then, because I can't help myself, I look around his frame and search for the camel jacket and sweater. The stranger is no longer there. I blink several times, certain I imagined him. "Not dizzy at all," I say breathlessly. "Also, did you freaking growl at me a moment ago?"

With a frown, Breckin looks over his shoulder, then back at me. "Why would I growl at you?" His smile is too wide to be truthful. "Let's go."

Go? I look for Zara. She's already pulling her skates off from where she sits in a pile of snow.

"Where are we going?" I ask as Breckin moves forward. He tugs on my hand, propelling my skates into a glide.

"To my place. We'll drop Zara off at her car behind the square first."

"Why are we—"

"Vivie," he interrupts, "did I tell you to slow down?" he asks, and I stare stupidly. "When you were spinning, did I tell you to slow down?"

"Yes?" My tone is questioning, which is crazy, because he most certainly did. I heard him.

"No. No, I did not. I *thought* it, but I didn't speak it. I also didn't growl at you. Not out loud. I know better." He hurries his steps, dragging me behind him like a sled.

He didn't speak?

"You heard my thoughts, Viv. You also spun inhumanly fast, and you lit up like the Fourth of July when I walked into Coffee Haven earlier. I was going to ignore the angelic glow until later, but the other stuff—" He glances over his shoulder again. "Let's go back to my place, okay?"

I bite my tongue, holding my thoughts as I remove my skates and we walk through the park back to Breckin's Bronco. Zara doesn't protest the abrupt end of our day. *What in the world did he do to her?*

"Are you sure you don't want to go to Rowan's party tonight?" Zara asks, poking her head into the vehicle once we arrive back at the square and she climbs out.

A loud high school party or a quiet night, kissing in the new year with Breckin? *No brainer.* "A Bishop party?" I ask.

"I know it's not normally our thing, but we're seniors. Plus, I don't have a boyfriend to ring in the new year with. Hopefully, I can find a willing participant later."

Oh, my poor boy-crazy friend. Does she resent the place Breckin has taken up in my life in such a short time? I look at Breckin, a silent *Should we go?* plastered on my face.

"Yeah, not happening. Sorry." His tone says he's far from sorry.

Zara rolls her dark eyes with a resigned sigh, like she didn't expect any different. "Whatever. You kids be good then. Keep all that snogging to a minimum."

Breckin's arm stretches along the back of the seats, his fingers combing through my hair. "No promises."

Zara closes the car door with a grumble. "God, I need to find myself a boyfriend."

"Happy New Year, best friend," I call out my open window while she unlocks her car. She flips me off with a laugh as Breckin drives off.

"Okay, let's take it back now." I spit out the words the moment we leave the parking lot. Shifting in my seat, I angle my body Breckin's way. He's so calm. *How is he so calm?* My nails dig into my palms, I'm that freaked. "How did I read your mind? What do you mean I spun inhumanly fast? How in the heck am I glowing? Oh! And, you used compulsion on Z!"

"Vivie, breathe."

"Breathe?" I use the dashboard to brace myself. "I'm pretty sure people are going to question why I'm suddenly a human light bulb, Breckin. Zara already did."

He takes my hand, his fingers weaving between mine.

"Am I a light bulb?" There's a note of humor in his question.

"I'm not what you are," I counter. He doesn't reply. His cheek dents inward, like he's biting it. His silence unnerves me. "Breckin? Do you want to tell me what's going on?"

His shoulders twitch as he pumps my hand in his. I've seen that move before. He's trying to control the angel within. That can't be a good sign.

"What's going on is we're going back to my house, where I get you all to myself for the entire night."

I smile in spite of myself. "You get me to yourself every night, Breck."

The boy lives at my apartment. At first, it was because of the threat looming from the reaper, Sebastian. Now he does it because my mother works nights and he can. Being apart from Breckin is rare, and thanks to our soul connection, that's a good thing. Neither of us handles forced separation well. It's beyond what is normal for two teenagers who began dating three weeks ago. Then again, we're not normal teenagers. He's part angel, and normal went out the window for me on the day I died. Well, died and was brought back to life by his angelic healing.

Breckin removes his hand from mine and adjusts the heater as we turn onto Eleventh. "Yes, but tonight I get you at my place, without having to worry about your mom coming home early from her shift." He holds his hand in front of me, testing the heat blowing from the vent. It's the sort of thing he does without even realizing it. "Did you call her today?"

Frustration wells up at his change of subject, but I indulge him. For now. "Yeah, earlier, while I was waiting on Zara at Coffee Haven. She's enjoying herself."

"And she's with college friends?" he asks.

I nod. "A few nursing school friends she's kept in touch with, yeah. They get together every year for a girls' weekend in Vegas."

"She trusts you."

"She's never had a reason not to. She's a single mom, so I learned to be responsible at a young age." I catch his small smile out of the corner of my eye. He knows what I'm saying. He didn't have parents growing up. He had nannies, and he had Elias.

"Does she trust me?" he asks.

"You're a guy. Of course she doesn't trust you." I laugh. "But she likes you enough, and she likes Elias. When she left yesterday, she gave me 'the talk.'"

The car slows as we near Breckin's house. "The talk? Vivie, I don't want her to think—"

"She doesn't," I rush to soothe his worry. "Like I said, she trusts me. Breck, my mother got pregnant from a weekend tryst, and the guy disappeared. I've lived with that my entire life. I won't make the same mistake. She knows that."

Breckin sucks in a breath. We turn into his driveway and pull into the garage. It's not until he kills the engine and the garage door closes behind us that he speaks. "You know we're different than that, right? I could never walk away from you. Sex or not."

Talking about sex is awkward. How is it that Zara brought it up earlier, and now Breckin and I are discussing it again? *Note to self: if you can't talk about it without blushing, you should not be doing it.*

"Because we're soul bonded?" I ask, staring out the windshield at the impeccably organized garage wall in front of me.

His fingers touch my chin, turning my face his way. "What do you think?" he asks softly.

I unbuckle myself and wind a hand around his neck, bringing our lips together.

"I think you would never leave me because I'm your favorite couch pillow," I tease against his mouth.

"Something like that," he agrees, pressing his warm lips to mine again and again.

Breckin's house is a mansion compared to the apartment Mom and I live in. It's not as overwhelming as the homes in Havenwood Heights, but the fully renovated and modernized Victorian is expansive and impressive. Since my first visit, we've always spent our time here on the basement level. It's ridiculous to call the space a basement. It has everything we need: bathroom, kitchen, pool room, television, fireplace, comfy sofas. There's even a guest bedroom. Plus, it's underground. In the two weeks since our fight with Sebastian, Breckin hasn't let up his guard. It's like he's worried the reaper told others about us—a Nephilim with a soulmate—and being in the basement eases that worry.

We settle on the couch and watch an action movie marathon. I scoot down low on the seat and prop my blanket-covered legs on the footrest. Breckin sprawls out lengthwise with his head on my lap—I *am* his favorite pillow—and his feet hanging over the opposite arm rest.

"Have you seen your father since that night?" I ask randomly, halfway into movie two during a commercial break.

His attention turns from the television, stilling the hand I've been running through his smooth angelic hair. He shakes his head in the negative as he turns in my lap. "I would have told you if I had."

"Would you?" I ask, twirling a chunk of his bangs around my index finger.

"Viv?"

I push at his head. "You changed the subject in the car, and you're not telling me everything. What are you worried about?"

He pulls himself into a sitting position and combs his fingers through his mussed hair. "I don't *know* anything. Yes, I'm worried. I'm worried that Hamon will try to take you from me. That another reaper will appear, that something else might want you, like Sebastian did." His shoulders rise with a deep inhale. "Vivie, I'm worried I hurt you when I healed you, and we just don't know the repercussions yet. Then there's my eighteenth birthday and what that will mean for me, for you, for us." He scrubs his hand over his face, and his shoulders drop. "Elias is keeping things from me."

I pull my legs in and set my feet on the floor. My arms and hands reach for Breckin, drawing him close, until he's the one wrapping me in a hug.

"I'm sorry," I murmur into his neck. "You don't have to keep it to yourself. I'm part of this now. Let me in."

His hold tightens. "You're a high school senior. This is not what you need to deal with."

"So are you," I remind him, and he exhales. "I know, you're not normal, but guess what, Breck? Neither am I. Not anymore."

We separate, and my fingers go to my hair, twirling the ends nervously.

Breckin shakes his head with a grin. "No, you're not. You were glowing today, like an angel. I think my healing you did something. Changed you somehow."

"You saved my life and made me your soul mate, but the

downside is I might be a human night-light?" When put in perspective, can I complain? So, I might glow occasionally. I could be dead.

"Elias trained me to control it, to mask it, when I was young. Maybe he could train you, too. We'll figure this out, but not tonight, Vivie." He gives my knee a squeeze, his amber eyes scanning my face. "Hey, you wanna go see the fireworks in a way you never have?"

I release my fear. He's so earnest. So worried about providing me with normal experiences, as though he's to blame for where we are now. "With you? Of course."

We take to the sky, leaving crowds and traffic jams to the humans. Every New Year's Eve Mount Mae Ski Resort has a torchlight parade down the blue square slope, Renae's Way. I've been many times, but never like this—never hidden in the sky, in the arms of an angel. From up here, the mountain appears like it's on fire. Skiers weave their way back and forth, the flames in their hands lighting the path, creating a radiance that steals your breath.

"It's pretty amazing, huh?" Breckin whispers in my ear.

"It's gorgeous," I agree. "This is why you love flying so much, isn't it? Everything is beautiful from up here. Lights look romantic, streets seem peaceful, the air is clean."

His wings stretch out, bringing us higher and moving us away from the slopes. "I used to love it because it cleared my head. Like running for you."

Like running *was* for me. Since the attack, I haven't been able to run. Haven't wanted to.

"You said used to," I point out, as below us the crowd erupts in a countdown.

His warm nose nudges the side of my face, pulling my attention from the ground to his eyes. "Isn't it obvious? I don't need to clear my mind the way I used to. When I'm stressed, I have you."

"Aw, of course you would say sweet things when I don't dare move."

Breckin laughs as a cannon pops in the distance. "I'll be sure to repeat myself when we're on the ground, then," he says, his leg hooking around mine tightly as he turns toward the north. Sparks ignite the sky, sizzling and popping in brilliant flashes.

"Happy New Year, Vivie."

Lifting my face to his, I smile as his eyes light up in a rainbow of colors. "Happy New Year, Breck," I say, my lips brushing his.

Purchase *Avenge the Heart* by Michele G. Miller at your favorite book retailer.